D0629866

WOLFPACK

ALSO BY AMELIA BRUNSKILL

The Window

WOLFPACK

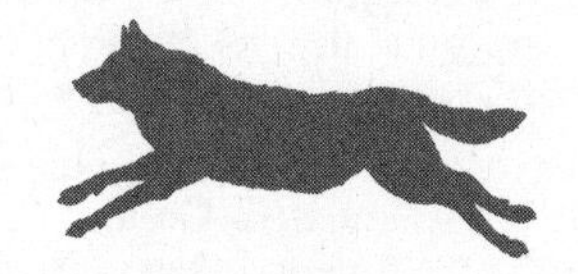

Amelia Brunskill

LITTLE, BROWN AND COMPANY
New York Boston

Interior design by Carla Weise.

Little, Brown and Company
Hachette Book Group
1290 Avenue of the Americas, New York, NY 10104
Visit us at LBYR.com

First Edition: June 2023

Library of Congress Cataloging-in-Publication Data
Names: Brunskill, Amelia, author.
Title: Wolfpack / Amelia Brunskill.
Description: First edition. | New York ; Boston : Little, Brown and Company, 2023. | Audience: Ages 14 & up. | Summary: A group of teenage girls living in a cult are ensnared by suspicion and paranoia when one of them goes missing.
Identifiers: LCCN 2022026026 | ISBN 9780316494557 (hardcover) | ISBN 9780316494809 (ebook)
Subjects: CYAC: Novels in verse. | Missing children—Fiction. | Loyalty—Fiction. | Murder—Fiction. | Communal living—Fiction. | Cults—Fiction. | LCGFT: Novels in verse.
Classification: LCC PZ7.5.B78 Wo 2023 | DDC [Fic]—dc23
LC record available at https://lccn.loc.gov/2022026026

ISBNs: 978-0-316-49455-7 (hardcover), 978-0-316-49480-9 (ebook)

Printed in the United States of America

LSC-C

Printing 1, 2023

To my parents, who I adore.

(I promise that you inspired absolutely none of what follows.)

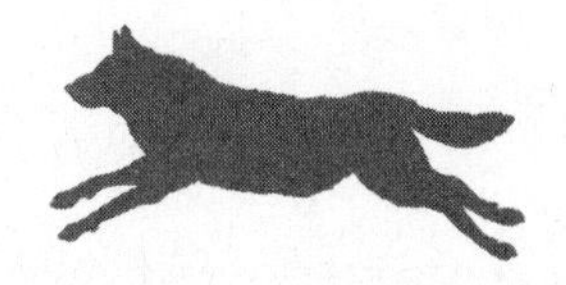

Other than the road that winds
along the west
Havenwood's boundaries
are not well defined.
To the north, are the woods
to the east, the river
and in neither do outsiders
ever set foot.
The one fence we have
is small and made of wood
serving only to protect our orchard
from overly bold deer.

The porous nature of Havenwood is intentional—
Joseph picked this place
knowing it had been waiting
to be reborn
into a vision,
an idea,
that could flow like water.

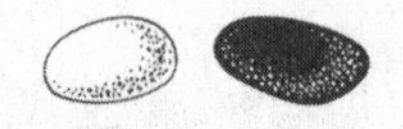

THE NINE OF US WERE NOT ALWAYS AS WE ARE NOW:
a group, a collective.
We were merely part of the larger scrum—
toddlers to almost full grown—
housed in the children's lodge.

Then four years ago
a blizzard came rushing through
and toppled a massive oak tree.
The tree ripped through the lodge's roof—
its branches extending down as if to caress our faces.
Only the youngest of the children cried out in fear.
The rest simply stared
at the suddenly visible sky—
waiting for a message from God.

The blizzard continued to rage
for days and days
and the nine of us girls
—then aged ten through fourteen—
were placed
in a shedlike structure
previously used for storage.

It was supposed to be
a temporary solution
yet soon we began to think of the structure
as our place—our cabin
and we found that we liked
being away from the boys,
the small children,
being able to do as we pleased,
be that slipping gently into silence
at the end of the day
or talking long into the night.

So we decided that we would be loyal
not just to Havenwood
but also to one another
and we shed our old names like snake skins
and tied ourselves together
by giving ourselves new names,
ones from the natural world:

Daisy

Fern

Ivy

Laurel

Oleanna

Poppy

Rose

Violet

Willow

And when the elders finally summoned us
to rejoin the others,
things had shifted
in a way that they had not seen coming
in a way that they did not approve
for together we felt
for the very first time
that we could say no.

Violet

At times, Violet has a sixth sense
one that draws her attention
to things not noticed by others.
This morning though
she feels nothing but the simple pleasure
of being outside in the shivery air
alone with her thoughts and her bees.

She hums quietly to herself
as she tucks the gloves into her sleeves,
adjusts her beekeeper's veil,
and picks up the smoker.
She does all this despite secretly believing
it's no longer necessary—
she's developed immunity
due to frequent initial stings
and, besides,
the bees are used to her now.
Still, she must be careful of the example she sets—
the children lust after honeycomb

so any hint that the bees do not warrant caution
could swiftly lead to tears.

As she walks toward the hives
she feels a smile grow on her face
and her heart rate slow.
She feels connected to the bees
has dreams where she is winged and aloft,
soaring above the compound,
seeking the sweetness of flowers.
Sometimes in these dreams
she is joined by
wide-eyed, tiny Daisy
or titian-haired Poppy—
or—
well—
there are other
more enticing, and less serene,
versions of this dream.

A bee lands on the sleeve of her suit
and starts to crawl up toward her cuff.
She pauses, and watches it,
amused by its dogged progress.
Some describe bees as automatons
attuned only to their prescribed role
and their queen's bidding

yet this bee seems driven
not by the promise of nectar or pollen
but by simple curiosity.

After it flies off
she continues on to the hives
where she applies
a soft wave of smoke.
She is reaching to pull out a frame
when something on the ground catches her eye:
a small pile of dead bees.
They'd stung something—attacked—
their efforts leaving their stingers gone,
their lower bodies torn open.

She steels herself
for the aftermath of an overnight siege.
Yet when she pulls out a frame
all she finds are smoke-dazed bees
blissfully unaware
that any larger danger might have passed by.

Ivy

IVY WAKES WITH THE FAINT ECHO
of an unexpected sound
still ringing in her head
one that caused her to briefly surface,
hours earlier.
She tries to coax it back,
but it has vanished—shy.

She is, as per often,
running behind,
and some of the girls have already left
—Oleanna is not there to braid her hair
and Rose is also away,
probably off badgering Violet
to give her some honeycomb.
Those remaining are almost dressed—
Laurel lacing her boots,
Daisy pinning up her hair into a pale wreath
Willow buttoning up a heavy cardigan.
Ivy had meant to wash this morning

but the lodge will be too crowded now
and Willow's cardigan indicates
a day too cold
to use the outdoor shower.

Could you please hand me some clothes? Some socks?
Ivy tosses out to the room,
with a wide, lazy smile,
hoping to snare someone into allowing her
to avoid exposing her bare feet to the chilled floor.
Usually, she might have luck with Willow or Daisy
but Laurel sends a stern look Ivy's way.
Just get up. It's almost breakfast.
The others then quickly avert their gaze,
not wanting to cross the line Laurel has drawn
but also knowing that, like her namesake,
Ivy has a way of encircling people
with her smile, her voice, wrapping around them
until they confuse her desires with their own.

Ivy reluctantly admits defeat
and as she rises, she asks,
Were any of you woken up earlier?
By an odd sound?
The other girls look at one another and shrug.
I don't think so, Daisy says.
Willow pauses, her eyes solemn.

I heard a whisky jack quite early.
Might it have been that?
Ivy shakes her head.
The sound had been flinty, she thinks,
metallic, even—not the call of a bird.
Laurel looks impatient
as if she suspects
not entirely incorrectly
that Ivy is now
simply stalling.
And so while it is tempting to press
the matter further
she is hungry
and so she lets it go.

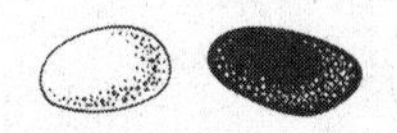

As we walk to breakfast
the thick mud alongside the path
speaks of heavy overnight rain
and we are surrounded by a thick mist
that transforms Havenwood's usual crisp beauty
into a landscape painted
with fatly dabbed brushstrokes.
Yesterday was much warmer, brighter,
and the shift leaves us disoriented.

It's Tuesday, so as we enter the main hall,
we expect to be greeted
by the smell of warm butter and salt
to see
women in aprons behind the long oak table
wielding gleaming silver ladles
ready to pour gravy onto steaming biscuits.

Instead there are no women in aprons
and all we see on the table
are bowls of cereal, dried fruit, and yogurt.

There are murmurs about a broken oven
confirmed by the sight of Fern
already seated at our table,
looking woebegone
her arms (for once) not dusted with flour.

Oleanna arrives just before the morning prayer
and as she scrapes her pale hair away from her face
we see swirls of brown ink
decorating the backs of her hands.
We try not to be envious:
We know it's hardest for Laurel,
we know she was hoping to be invited
to join Joseph's prayer circle
but clearly her hope has gone unmet.

Fern sighs. *I was going to make pies today,*
perhaps to provide a needed distraction,
and the loss of these pies is indeed a diversion,
a turned knife in our culinary wound.
What kind of pies? Violet asks.
Apple and blackberry, Fern replies.
Some meat pies too—
there's a potential coming today.
We nod—Joseph likes us to greet potentials
with a feast
to show off our bounty.

He'll be disappointed that the ovens
have let us down.
When Poppy shows the potential around
she'll have to charm them enough
to render the pies unnecessary.

When everyone is seated,
there can briefly be heard
the soft ripple
of almost two hundred people
adjusting in their seats
before a perfect hush falls over the room
as Joseph takes his place at the podium.

It's true that Joseph's power
stems from how he founded Havenwood
how he took his millions earned in tech
and created a place of salvation here
but it also comes from
how he knows everything about us,
even things we barely knew ourselves,
how he looks like a Viking king
with chiseled jaw and silver mane.

Like all mornings
Joseph thanks us for our work,
 thanks God for the abundance of the harvest

thanks the flowers and the bees
the weather, the sun
the stars.
When he stops, we lower our heads
observe two minutes of perfect silence
in which not so much as a fork is shifted.

When he rings the silver bell
we all raise our heads—
except Daisy, whose neck briefly stays bent,
her eyelids closed.
It's understandable—
the abrupt change in weather
has fogged our senses,
and staying upright takes
more effort than usual.

Surely this is the reason why
only some of us
notice the empty chair at our table
and no one comments on it.

Poppy

THE POTENTIAL—HELEN—
is only a few years older than Poppy herself
but has a young baby,
still in arms.

Usually Poppy's role
is simply to put the potential at ease
with her bright, personable manner
but as Poppy shows Helen around the grounds
it becomes clear
there have been considerable omissions
in this woman's briefing.

Yes, Helen was told Havenwood's origin story:
How several decades ago
a tornado swept through this expanse of farmland
decimating much of the area, yet leaving
the structure that's now the meetinghouse
perfectly untouched.
How Joseph saw a photo of it in the newspaper,

and instantly understood it as a sacred place
one he purchased in cash
the very next day.

And, yes, Helen has also been informed
of the most basic of Havenwood's tenets:
She will never be able to lie with someone here
that alcohol is forbidden except on solstice
that she has three weeks to decide whether to stay
but leaving after that means
she can never return
and her soul will not be saved.

But Helen has not been told
many of the other important details
how here nothing is wasted or thrown away
how everyone must contribute their time and talents
how no communication with the outer world is allowed.
So Poppy must instead be the one
to fill in these blanks.

Fortunately, Helen seems unworried
by any of the new intel
less concerned about whether
she'll want to stay
than if she might be forced to leave.

When Helen asks nervously about unwelcome visitors
Poppy tells her of their system for gathering together
how a bell is rung, and weapons made ready
but assures her such visitors are rare.
It does not seem important
to mention the one several weeks earlier—
in which only voices
not rifles
had been raised.

In the orchard,
Poppy switches to light conversation
complimenting the long gray scarf
wrapped high around Helen's neck
the one item of Helen's clothing
she can realistically admire.

Thank you, Helen says, pleased.
I love your sweater.

Thank you, Poppy says.
I made it myself.

It's beautiful, Helen says,
admiring the thick knit.
Did you learn that here?

Yes. I learned everything here.
I arrived here very young,
too young to remember anything from before.

It was a blessing, she knows,
to have avoided the pain of those
—like Fern—
denied this place
until damage was already done
to instead still be so young
that it was easy to dissolve
the bonds of blood
and in their place
form strong
communal roots.

Even without her vocalizing this
Helen seems to understand
responding by looking down at her child
with glistening eyes
and Poppy sends out a silent hope
that Havenwood will work out
for this woman, this child
that Helen will not be one
who never acclimates as they should
nor one who betrays it,
like Michael.

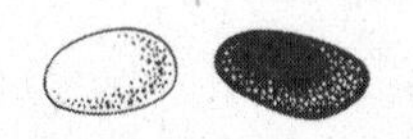

Naturally, Poppy was right
to be somewhat disconcerted
by how little Helen had been told
—this is not how it should have been—
yet in truth
there are things about us
about Havenwood
that we intentionally
don't tell potentials.
Things that require
more time
more context.

Some, like the matching scars
lining our lower backs, the tops of our legs
are easily avoided—
we simply don't reveal these parts of ourselves
circumventing the need to explain
that the caning
was a punishment
we were happy to endure
for our decision to leave the lodge.

Other things, we keep out of sight
like the keys around our necks
which we tuck into our necklines.
Because Havenwood is supposed to have
no barriers or divisions
yet the door to our cabin has a lock
with nine identical keys
due to a man who once lived among us
a man who once entered our cabin
while Daisy was sleeping alone
the unbuckling of his belt only interrupted
by the return of Laurel and Poppy.

The rock circle we cannot conceal
but we are very careful
when directly asked
about how
we frame its function.
Not lying, no,
but leaving much unsaid.
Still, it always surprises us
how few potentials even think to inquire
about what purpose it serves.

Willow

WILLOW VOLUNTEERS TOO SWIFTLY
after Violet asks the group
who wishes to join her
in foraging for mushrooms.
She blushes at her own haste
worried others will note
her uncharacteristic interest
in venturing into the woods
that Rose, perhaps, will remark on it
in a manner less than kind.

When she glances around, however,
she finds that Rose is absent
and none of the others appear
to have registered anything amiss.
Willow is relieved, pleased at the thought
she has perhaps been successful
in concealing her fear of wild places—
not wanting to be teased about being

only comfortable in places like the library,
where she organizes the books,
places small, confined, and orderly
the kind of girl
who'd never stray from a path.

She and Violet are only a few yards in,
the sun's light still reaching them unfettered
before Violet reaches out
and silently pulls Willow's hand into hers,
threading her fingers
through Willow's
and then squeezing softly.

I'm so glad you came, but I didn't
expect you to volunteer, Violet says.
Will you be all right?

Yes, I just wish I'd worn another layer,
Willow says.
And in perfect Violet fashion
Violet immediately begins to unwind
the scarf from her own neck
again proving she is so innately good
that surely nothing she does
could ever truly be wrong.
No, really, Willow says with a smile,
I'll be fine.

This she thinks but leaves unsaid:
You will, I know,
find other ways
to keep me warm.

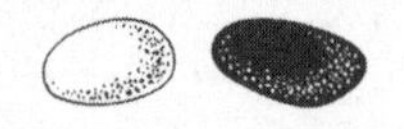

Usually Joseph presides over
the last bonfire of the season
but perhaps he is drained
from a long night of communing
with his inner circle
because tonight he is absent.

Instead, it is Sarah
—Joseph's familiar—
who rises to make the speech
and as she speaks
we let our eyes and thoughts slightly wander.

It's not that Sarah is unimposing—
her blond hair transitioning seamlessly into white
her diction crisp, befitting her trial-lawyer past—
but she is not Joseph.
No, Sarah is not our leader
she is instead a lieutenant
noticing things, tending to things
that may require handling
with a certain skill.
We suspect that ever since

we refused to return to the lodge
we've become one of the things Sarah notices
one of the things she monitors.

When Sarah ends her speech
the children disperse from their tight group
beelining for their preferred target.
While Poppy is the most favored
equally for her warm demeanor and vibrant hair
some children attach to others of us
such as beautiful, vivacious Ivy,
or gentle Violet, who smells of beeswax and honey,
while a few children instead sit at a respectful distance
from a cluster of the older boys.

For years, we slept in the lodge with these boys
studied with them, learning to write and read
their studies continuing after ours ended.
When we left the lodge,
some, like Hamish, were stoic
about the change
while others, like Zachary, deeply resented
being robbed of the pleasant certainty
that someone else would tend to a child's
frantic midnight terror
or mumbled shame over wet sheets.
There is an irony

we sometimes quietly think
that after being asked so long
to act like adults, like mothers
we were treated like ungrateful children
when we stopped
while the boys, now men,
were treated like put-upon adults—
their greater physical strength apparently elevating them
past such lesser work.

One of the older boys, Jacob,
has a guitar case nestled at his feet,
when he leans down to unzip it,
we can't help but smile in anticipation:
his music and the showers are the only two things
we miss about the lodge.
He plays a folk song to which we all know the words
and our voices swell and drop together.

After a few songs, Jacob puts down his guitar
and the children demand
that Poppy tell them a story.
I don't know any stories, she teases them.
You do though, a child responds. *You do.*

Poppy relents and tells them one we know well
although usually it's Rose who tells it.

Poppy's version is less dark,
less gruesome than Rose's
resulting in a tale
both more palatable
and less engaging.

When she finishes, the children clamor for another.
Poppy laughs. *I'm going to roast a marshmallow.*
Have someone else tell you a story.
We instinctively all look for Rose:
We don't see her.
We quickly, silently, do a count:
Everyone else is here.

We all look to Fern
the one of us closest to Rose
but Fern shakes her head.

We know we must wait
until we are back in our cabin
to speak about this more.
For it's never a small thing to say
someone has gone missing—
but especially not when the last one
fled in the middle of the night
with a suitcase full of
Havenwood's money.

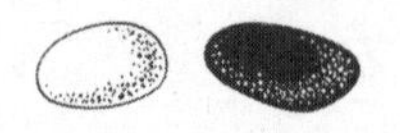

WHEN WE RETURN TO OUR CABIN
our clothes smoke saturated
our nerves raw
it is obviously empty.

Still, we do an inventory
find Rose's clothes in the closet,
her slippers by the door,
and the camera she constantly used—
a long-term loan from an elder—
on top of the chest of drawers.
We only have two versions each
of every item of clothing
two sweaters
two shirts
two dresses
two pairs of shoes
so we can quickly determine
Rose's only things missing:
a pair of shoes, a gray wool dress,
her thick wool sweater.
The only other thing we notice gone
is a small canvas bag

used for foraging.
If it wasn't long since dark
she might have simply gone out to pick
blackberries or dandelion greens.

Daisy is the one to say it out loud:
Do you think she left us?
The words prompt the rest of us to demur:
        Of course not.
        No.
        No, definitely not.
If she had, we proclaim
she would have told us,
or at least left a note,
        propped up on one of the pillows
                or on the chest of drawers,
                        or tacked to the door.
We ignore the whisper in our minds
that Rose could be thoughtless, rash
might not have taken
the time to write.

Perhaps she's in the infirmary? Ivy suggests.
She could have twisted her ankle
on the way to the darkroom?
Or tripped carrying too much laundry?

We nod eagerly
ashamed of not thinking of this possibility
before (silently) entertaining the idea
that she'd abandoned us.

Since curfew has descended
Daisy volunteers to check the infirmary
first thing tomorrow.
We relax, already imagining
Rose annoyed at us
for not finding her earlier,
for not bringing her a change of clothes
or perhaps a book.

Why didn't you look for me? she'll ask.
Did you really think I might have left?

No, we'll say. *Of course not.*

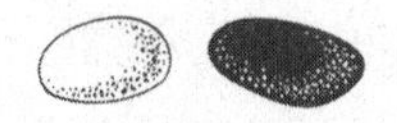

HAVENWOOD IS NOT A PLACE
that encourages any emphasis on blood ties.
Still, most of us know
the basic facts of our parentage.

Some are still here,
like Willow's father, who arrived a widower,
overwhelmed with grief.
Some choose to leave
like Laurel's young mother,
abandoning paradise and Laurel
for the dark thrills
of the wider world.
Some are no longer on this earth,
like Oleanna's parents—
killed on their very route to Havenwood
by a driver
drunk and careless on a blind turn.

Among us, only Rose's parentage
is a true mystery.
For Rose was brought here
as a very small child

by a man, haggard and wild-eyed,
    who claimed to be her uncle
and then disappeared.

We made up origin stories for her—
taking pieces from legends and fairy tales
and shaping them together.
She had the beauty and bearing of a princess,
regal and sure
with a quick tongue
that dealt out harsh truths
so we made her the heir
of a cruel king and a beautiful queen
of a mad fairy and a noble knight
wrapping her in layers of beautiful nonsense
that we spun around and around.

We thought her satisfied
by these invented histories,
until one night she'd posed a question
to the dark of the room
asking why no one had ever come for her.
It's not like I'd go with them, she'd said,
a quaver in her voice.
But shouldn't they want to know?
Shouldn't someone be looking for me?
None of us had an answer,

so we'd curled around her, stroked her hair
massaged her feet.

It was a night we'd think back on later
to remind ourselves
that she could be hurt
just as she, sometimes,
hurt us.

Daisy

DAISY FEELS CLEAR THIS MORNING, PURPOSEFUL—
glad to have claimed the task of checking
for Rose at the infirmary.
She hopes this will help her
start to extricate herself
from the role she's fallen into—
the whiny youngest, or
as Rose once phrased it:
Our hapless baby child.

Daisy cuts through the orchard,
making use of the gaps between the rows.
The trees are planted in neat lines,
yet their limbs arch out wildly,
clutching for one another.
Many are already heavy with apples,
but others only have small, tight knots.

There will come a time in the late autumn
when she will be sick of apples—

when she will despise their sweetness.
For now though she has to hold herself back
from filling her pockets with them,
from letting her teeth sink into their tender flesh.

On the outside, the infirmary looks desolate,
almost abandoned
a heap of lumber stacked beside it
for a long-delayed extension.
Inside though
it's modern and pristine,
tiled with sleek white ceramic.

Clara, the nurse on duty,
is reading a book.
She glances up when Daisy enters
giving her a quick, slightly quizzical smile.

I wasn't expecting you until this
afternoon, Clara says.

After breakfast, I'm going foraging,
Daisy replies. *Do you need anything?*
Clara frowns, thinking.

Yarrow. Also, pick some sage from
the garden—we keep running short.

Shall I check in the back to see
if anything else is low?

Yes. Do it quietly though—
we have one who's had two
rough nights.

When Clara's eyes drop back to her book
Daisy moves past,
letting her gaze wander across the beds.
One contains a man,
or possibly boy,
with dark, damp hair clinging to his neck.
Another contains a younger girl
one who'd once knocked on their door
and shyly asked to join them—
a request that was gently rebuffed
—it was already bold enough
for them to have left the lodge
they could not risk it being believed
they were recruiting others away.

Moving toward the suite at the back,
Daisy pauses briefly in front of the tidy row
of glass jars
yarrow and sage are low
but all the others are filled high.

Her eyes flick to Clara
still reading

and then she takes steps toward the suite
peers through the window.

Both beds are neatly made,
with white sheets tightly tucked
and a light blue blanket folded in a square.
And both are empty.

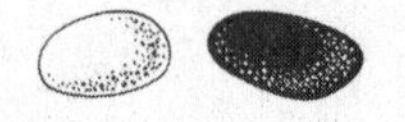

THE REST OF US ARE ALREADY IN LINE FOR BREAKFAST—
eyeing the tall stacks of pancakes and bacon—
when Daisy comes into the meeting hall.
We raise our eyebrows in unison
waiting for her to release our tension
with a smile and nod.
Instead she offers up
a tight shake of her small head.

We pause—blindsided.

Rose is gone, missing.
She has left us,
probably,
yes.
Left us without
so much as a note.

A woman behind us
clears her throat noisily
indicating that the line has moved
we force ourselves to shuffle forward
to fill the gap.

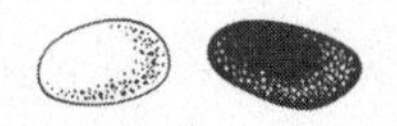

OUR ATTENTION IS SPLIT
as Joseph says his blessing—
and we feel no small guilt for this—
with Sarah often now leading the evening prayer
many days this morning prayer
is the only one we will receive from him.

We remain quiet even after the bell rings
and for once the food holds no pleasure for us.
Still, we try to clear our plates
as best we can—
too much uneaten food could draw
unwanted attention.

Afterward, we congregate outside,
standing near the circle
with its ring of stacked stones.

Rose might not have left on purpose.
She might be hurt, or lost in the
woods, Daisy says, her voice
nervous and high.

Rose won't have gotten lost,
Violet says. *She knows the woods too well.*

But what if she did, or what if
someone—

Daisy's fingers wrap themselves around
the key that dangles from her neck,
and unconsciously we all grasp ours too—
silently reminding ourselves that the man
who tried to hurt Daisy
will never return.
No, Laurel says firmly but gently.
I'm sure that's not what happened.

Should we tell Joseph? Ivy asks.
Or Sarah?

If we do, there will be questions
about whether she can come back,
Willow says quietly.

We'd take her back though,
wouldn't we? Daisy asks.
If she changes her mind?

Some of us nod
Some of us hesitate.
There is no easy consensus here.
For while not telling of Rose's absence
doesn't precisely break a rule,
allowing someone to return to Havenwood does
and could, like all rule-breaking,
result in the universe doling out consequences
either to the rule-breaker themselves

or someone they cared about
in unsettling
and unexpected ways.

If we don't tell, someone would need
to cover for her chores,
Poppy says, her tone neutral,
advocating neither for
nor against this idea.

I could do the laundry for her,
Daisy offers. *I don't mind.*

But what if someone asks about her?
Violet asks.

We could go with what we
originally thought happened—
that she twisted her ankle,
Willow says. *We could say she's*
recuperating in bed.

It is startling to hear it out loud—
the idea of actively lying
to protect Rose.

As usual, Laurel rallies first, and takes charge,
forming our most immediate quandary
into a clear choice:
Should we tell?
We each reach into our pockets

for the two pebbles we keep there—
black for no, white for yes.
Everyone must place a vote, eyes closed.

We select our decision,
and then one by one
we transfer them into Laurel's hand.
When she opens her hand, we see
five black pebbles, three white:
At least for now,
Rose's absence will be our secret.

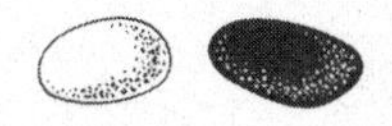

THERE'S A PHOTO
we made Rose take of us all
after we'd woven flowers in our hair
put on our favorite dresses.

She shot us in the meadow
when the sun hovered low in the sky
brushing the edges of the grass and our limbs
golden soft.
Poppy made all these dresses
except for the one Ivy is wearing,
a sheath with a lace panel in front,
a discard from an elder.

We've read books about
groups of girls
going to a big school dance,
and that's what this picture makes us think of—
smiling, laughing, waiting to go somewhere,
all dressed up.
Looking at it, we can imagine that
after Rose clicked the shutter
we all walked out to the road,

piled into a long car
that drove off
as soon as the last of us
had pulled the door closed.

Not that there is anywhere
that we would wish to go.
Remaining in the cabin
was our one rebellion
earning us both
the sharp pain
of Joseph's cane against our legs
and a freedom, a resolve
that formed its own version
of scar tissue.

Oleanna

Oleanna sits beside Ivy at a long wood table
and together they tackle the pile of mail—
Ivy sorting the unopened mail
and Oleanna opening any personal correspondence
and assessing if it warrants a response.

Oleanna knows her own role
is a critical one
based on great personal trust
earned by her unswerving devotion
to Havenwood and all it stands for.
Ivy's role is instead
a form of containment
intended to protect others from the lure
of her excessive lashes, cascading dark hair,
and the tendrils of her low voice
which turns even the simplest of phrases
into a beguiling promise.

And Ivy is, as ever, moving slowly
her movements relaxed
whereas Oleanna has already read
through eight letters:
five inquiries from potentials
three letters from family members in the outer world
who do not seem to have accepted
that they will be receiving no answer.

The potentials write about wanting
meaning and purpose,
of being overwhelmed, afraid
of the direction of the larger world
of long searching for a place like Havenwood
where they can feel useful
safe.
These letters serve to steady Oleanna
reminding her of how important this place is
how essential it is
that its rules be followed.

She scans the letters from family members
for threats and then again for notable details.
In these there are no threats
only pleas for a response.
One letter mentions a childhood memory
a sailboat adventure

with salt air and bologna sandwiches.
Oleanna jots that down
and then tosses the letter into the trash
as trained.

A small sound of irritation from Ivy
redirects Oleanna's attention,
to Ivy holding an envelope with smudged ink
squinting, and trying to make out the name
to whom it is addressed.
Oleanna makes a sharp gesture for it
wanting it out of Ivy's grasp,
and Ivy, unimpressed, hands it over.

For Oleanna,
the handwriting is perfectly legible
and as she stares at it,
for a moment
or perhaps two
the world goes a quiet dark
like she's being held underwater.
In the space of a long breath
she surfaces
and in the space of another
she slips the envelope
deep into her pocket.

My Dear One,

I'm sorry. I've started this letter a million times, a million ways, but in the end that's what I keep coming back to, the only thing that truly matters.

If you read no further, please know this is the simple truth: I'm so very sorry.

Laurel

At midday, Laurel climbs a tree
at the edge of the woods
climbing as far up as she can
hoping from this height
she'll see Rose making her way back
having found whatever she was seeking.

She suspects the others
assume she selected a white pebble
—voted to tell the elders about Rose—
a reasonable guess, given her usual tendency
to narrowly interpret Havenwood's rules
and shepherd the group
firmly within them.

However, in actual fact,
she'd selected a black one
without hesitation.
A few weeks earlier,
she'd seen Rose staring

with a wistful expression
at a magazine photo of mothers with their children
and Laurel now wishes she'd spoken up
told Rose not to romanticize blood ties
not to risk losing the paradise
both on Earth and eternal
only Havenwood provides.
She could have reminded Rose
of how Laurel's own mother
had left her in Havenwood
leaving behind
only a legacy of shame.

From her high vantage point
she can see
the pottery shed where she'd spent the morning
the cows grazing in the pasture
the long, dense expanse of the woods
the stony shore of the glinting river
but no Rose.

Laurel sighs,
and takes her sandwich from her pocket.
She's four bites in
when she hears movement at the base of the tree
and sees through the leaves
Poppy's vermilion crown.

Some would wait for permission
before climbing up
but Poppy and Laurel have done this
many times before,
eaten together,
gently processing their thoughts.

When Poppy reaches Laurel,
she straddles a sturdy branch
and scans the horizon.

I looked too, Laurel says. *She's not there.*

Do you think she's left for good?
Poppy asks.

No, I suspect she'll be back before long.

I hope you're right.

For a time
they silently eat together
pretending not to be watching
for Rose to appear.
She does not.
Instead, in the distance,
it is Joseph and Zachary who come into view,
walking close together
with perfectly matched strides.
Zachary is only a few years older than Laurel,
they'd learned sums and reading together

in the renovated barn.
He'd usually had the right answer
and quietly seethed
when she had it first.

Joseph's been spending a lot of time
this year with Zachary,
Poppy says.

Yes. And also with Hamish.
It seems like Joseph's settled
on the two of them.

Hamish makes sense.
Everyone likes him—even the
animals.
He'd be the easy choice, surely.

Zachary's smarter though—
you know how Joseph values that.

Not smarter than you.

While Laurel appreciates the compliment
they both know
her own intelligence
is besides the point.
Joseph would never have considered
any of the girls as protégés—
even Sarah was treated
more as a trusted placeholder
than a true leader.
Of course, a succession could be decades away,

she says, her conscience suddenly pricked
for having even indulged in such discussion.
Joseph still has greater strength and speed
than many half his age.

Of course, Poppy acknowledges.
And in the meantime, he really
should invite you to the prayer
circle.

Maybe he feels he only needs one of us,
Laurel says, as lightly as she can.

Only one, and he picks Oleanna?

She's completely loyal.
Always follows the rules.

Certainly, she's perfect if he wants
a sheep.
But to protect his herd,
he also needs wolves.

After a brief guilty silence
they both begin to laugh
a giddy, innocent release to a stressful day.
Because Oleanna is no sheep
and Laurel is, of course, no wolf.

Fern

FERN WAS IN THE OUTSIDE WORLD
many years longer
than any of the others.
Occasionally, she allows herself
to think about things about it
she could almost make herself miss:
Movie theaters, with screens so large,
and sound from everywhere at once.
Escalators, where she trailed her hand along the side
as she glided upward.
Vending machines packed
with terrible, delicious choices.
Most of the time though
she doesn't let herself think about these things.
She lets them vanish, eclipsed—
as they should be, as they were—
by all the bad things:
The dirt that was never only soil,
but crumpled trash and cigarette butts
and refuse of a million kinds.

The smell of old urine under the bridges,
The embarrassed, angry expression on people's faces
that half-second before they looked away.

She is worried about Rose—
worried for Rose.
She'd voted to tell
not believing
that Rose left of her own accord.
She wishes she'd spoken up, argued her case,
but it had gone so fast
before she'd managed to organize
her thoughts into words.

She'd told Rose about the outside world,
seen on Rose's face
no traces of interest, of yearning.
The others, she knows,
think of Rose
as being as careless about this place
as she was with her words—
remembering how she'd
snapped at Ivy for her tuneless humming
told Violet off for talking too much about her bees
teased Daisy for being whiny and indecisive.
But while Rose lashed out
letting her words leave marks

Fern knows Rose truly loved the group
loved Havenwood
and so she believes
in the very marrow of her bones
that Rose did not mean to stay away.

Violet

IT'S BEFORE DAWN
on the fourth day of Rose's absence
and the sky is still mulberry dark
as Violet quietly pulls on her boots
trying to ensure that none of the others stir.
Before she leaves, she glances at Willow,
gently sleeping,
and she fights the temptation to step backward
and carefully brush Willow's hair from her face.

The outside air is damp and chilled
and she hugs her arms tightly to herself
and tries to walk fast to get warm.

She's almost reached the woods
when she spies a clothed form
tucked around the base of a tree.
Her heart pounds—*Rose*—
before her brain computes

first that the form is male
and second that it belongs to Peter,
an elder, curled in sleep.
Even with his river-blue eyes shut
Peter is handsome
yet in this moment he has a smell to him
high and rank.

Alcohol is forbidden
on any day other than the summer solstice
and such a blatant infraction should be
immediately reported
but Violet wavers,
remembering the story
quietly circulated about Peter's before times:
a tale of a young wife and child
who drowned in the ocean
tugged down deep and swift
by a fierce current
on a perfect summer day.

She casts her gaze around
to see if she is being observed.
Seeing no one
she keeps moving forward.

The woods fold her into their darkness
with the heavy wet smell of moss and decaying leaves.
She wishes she could go without the flashlight,
slink like an animal through the trees,
but she is forced to switch it on.

She is out here
because she knows how to find
the places of the others,
where they hide their small secrets.
She doesn't mean to know these things,
she just accumulates telltale details
the dusting of barn-attic red
along Oleanna's arm
the smell of birch sap clinging to Laurel
when she's claimed to be throwing pots all day—
details that do not demark a specific location
but, for Violet, provide enough to narrow it down,
to make the finding a simple technicality to overcome.

This gift is not one she uses lightly—
she does not like to trespass—
but Rose's absence is now long enough
she feels obligated to see if it can
shed some light
on Rose's intentions.

The beam of light follows the map
she'd sketched out in her head,
based on a memory of meeting Rose
along this path:
Rose with a furtive look on her face
red clay dirt on her dress's hem
a stray oak leaf clinging to her sleeve.

Violet winds her way around
until she comes to a patch of red earth
in front of an oak tree with a deep hollow.
Her fingertips push into it,
the wood soft and crumbly,
until they encounter resistance.

One by one, she brings out Rose's things:
three items that she chose to hide away
that Rose did not want to share,
things she wanted to have as her own.
Things surely Rose would have taken with her,
had she planned to leave forever.

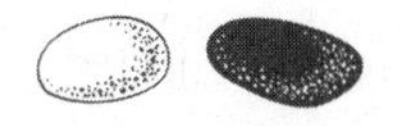

THE FIRST TO ASK US ABOUT ROSE
is neither an elder nor a contemporary
but instead a small, towheaded girl
who'd always sat close
when Rose had told stories.

She approaches us after breakfast
and we tell her about Rose's ankle
how Rose is resting in bed
how we are bringing her meals to her.
Like all of us, this child has been trained
not to ask too many questions
yet she meets our answer with a skeptical gaze—
visibly unimpressed.
It's possible we fumbled our delivery
or perhaps it's simply a weak cover story
one quickly settled on
intended only to buy Rose a day or two
its plausibility now stretching thin.

Having used it once, we are stuck with it
but we quietly resolve to do better next time—
we'll roll our eyes as we say it

blame Rose for being overly dramatic
using a small injury
to get out of her chores.
We will sound annoyed but unconcerned
and we will make them believe.

Willow

THE DOOR TO THE LIBRARY OPENS
with a soft whisper.
Willow expects to see one of the other girls,
asking her to recommend a book
or perhaps—she secretly hopes—
Violet slipping through
to snag a clandestine kiss.

Instead, it's Hamish
who usually wears a broad, confident smile
—radiating vigor and youth—
yet today he looks older and tired
like a version of himself in thirty years
is showing through thinned skin.
For a strange moment
he reminds her
of the man who was once her father
who now slides past her
like a ghost.

She castigates herself for such foolishness
and starts to rise from the table,
ready to assist.

Please don't get up on my account,
Hamish says, shaking his head.

Then he stands looking at the shelves,
his eyes roaming back and forth across the spines.
She doesn't remember seeing him here before
and the large scale of him
turns the room small.

Can I help you find something?

He glances at her.
Oh, I'm just looking for a book.

She smiles. *I'll need a bit more than that.*
There's a pause
a tick in time
when she worries she's misread
the situation.

He gives her a rueful smile.
It was leather-bound, red.
That's all I remember about it, I'm
afraid. And then he lets out a
long yawn.

Still tired after the prayer circle?
It's meant to be a joke, mostly—
the circle was several days ago now.

His eyebrows flick up for a second,
as if he is confused by her statement,
or perhaps he is simply surprised at her imprudence
in bringing up the prayer circle—
which is rarely explicitly discussed.

I'm just tired, he says.
I was ill recently, and it's taken me
longer than expected to recover.

She nods, fast
glad he graciously sidestepped
her unfortunate comment.
He pauses, and for a second,
she thinks he is about to change course
and ask for her assistance.
Instead, he shakes his head
and then silently leaves the room.

Fern

The ovens have been fixed
and Fern is relieved to be able to return
to what she loves, and does, best
to help distract her from thoughts of Rose.

A less welcome distraction
comes from the presence of Helen, the potential
who stands beside Fern, closer than she'd prefer,
braiding loaves of brioche.
Helen apparently worked in a bakery once
but Fern suspects Helen
did not work there long,
or it was not a good bakery,
for Helen had to be shown multiple times
how to roll out strands of dough
how to braid them together—
not too loose, not too tight.

Wanting to add some chopped chives
to the next batch of biscuits

Fern reaches for the knife block
only to find her preferred blade missing.
She starts to pivot toward the sink
where it is likely soaking
but finds Helen looking at her expectantly
as if awaiting an answer to a question.

Sorry, she says. *Did you say something?*
I was just saying I can't believe
how quiet it is here, Helen says.
Yes. Very quiet.
She tries to let her tone convey
that quiet is her preferred state.
But apparently Helen is immune
to such nuance.
I'm so used to having this constant
drone of traffic at all hours.
Out here there's almost no one on
the road at all. She smiles.
It must have been an easy place to
learn to drive.
I wouldn't know.
You don't drive?
No, none of us do.
None of the girls or women, I mean.
Helen frowns, as if recalibrating.

That can't be right. What about
that blond girl in the blue truck?

Daisy's hair is goldenrod
Oleanna's pale yellow
but neither drives
nor is there a vehicle here
matching that description.

Short hair? Truck a bit dented?

These details snap it into place.
That girl lives on the farm, past the woods.
Why did you think she was one of us?

She was parked on the other side
of the road the morning I arrived.

Fern absorbs this slowly.
That girl and her family
usually speed past Havenwood
as if afraid to linger.
Yet she was waiting in her truck
the morning Helen arrived
the same morning that
Rose disappeared.

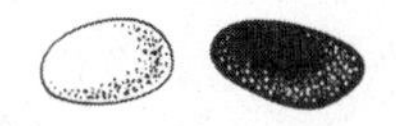

We don't know the name
of the girl who lives on the farm.
We know many other things though.
We know that she is tall and strong
lifts hay bales with ease
carries lambs with tender care.
She is older than us, but not much.

It's only a two-mile walk to her farm
if we go through the woods,
but it rained last night
leaving the ground churned up and muddy,
so we take the slightly longer route
through the fields.
We bring a jar of honey
as a small offering.

At the farm's fence
we pause before climbing over it.
On the other side, we join hands
and walk toward
the blue-painted house,

through tall rows of corn
rustling.

The door opens before we get there,
and the girl's father comes out.
He does not look pleased to see us.
You're from that place, he says.
With the weirdos.

Our faces tighten, but we nod.
We had a question, Poppy says.
For your daughter.
You're looking for Madison?
Privately, we judge this name and find it strange.
Still, Poppy manages to nod politely.
Yes. We think she might be able to help us
with something we lost.
Our cat, Violet adds.

He turns his head and
hollers out her name.
A clattering sound signals her descent down the stairs.
The smile on her face
drops
when she sees us.
She looks at us one by one,
searching, we realize, for Rose.

They're looking for their cat,
the man tells her.
Yes, she says. *I think I might have*
seen it.

She leads us into the barn
which is much newer than ours
and while some of the smells are the same,
others are sharp and abrasive.
We try not to flinch, to wrinkle our faces.
You're here about your friend Rose,
she says. *She asked me for a ride*
but never showed up.
Yes, Laurel says.
Where did she want you to take her?
Into the city.
Did she tell you what for?
She just said she wanted to see it.
To take some photos.
Rose had not taken the camera
so we are not sure if we believe
Rose said this,
and we certainly do not believe
this was the actual reason
but we let it slide,
for now.

Was she supposed to meet you by the road?
Fern asks.

No, she said she'd come here.
When she didn't show, I thought
perhaps she'd overslept or been
delayed by the rainstorm.

Did she tell you anything else?
Were you going to bring her back?

She hesitates.
You find that cat? her dad calls out.

Yes, she calls back, sounding
grateful for the interruption.
They're about to leave.
Sorry, she tells us, *but you really*
should go. I can't tell you
anything more.

She scoops up a skinny tabby cat
and thrusts it forward.

Here, just let him loose when
you're past the fence.

Daisy is the first to extend her arms
and so in them Madison deposits
the limp, purring cat.
It proceeds to knead its head
against Daisy's throat.

You can also keep him if you want,
Madison says, smiling.
He's a terrible mouser.

The cat purrs in response
it seems that it and Daisy
have already made an agreement.

Before we go
we pause
wondering if we should ask Madison
to tell us if she hears from Rose.
But, no, we cannot believe
Rose would come back to her
instead of to us,
and asking would only
make us look weak.
So instead we simply hand Madison
the jar of honey
even though we are not entirely sure
she deserves it.

Poppy

Poppy does not go to dinner
that night.
She instead stays in the cabin
claiming that she feels unwell.
The trip to see Madison has unsettled her
left her with the sense
they'd been asking the wrong questions
that the girl had not trusted them enough
to tell them the whole truth
and held something back.

The idea that Rose would risk so much
for the sole purpose of taking photographs
is absurd
yet it occurs to her
she would have expected
—if Rose had intended to come back—
that Rose would have been unable to resist
taking the camera
so perhaps the fact that Rose hadn't

meant Rose had indeed not
intended to return.

Yet that doesn't sit right with her
for while Rose was not always easy—
was sometimes even borderline scornful
of the rules of this place
and those within it—
she was also so straightforward, so candid
that Poppy cannot imagine
Rose choosing to simply disappear forever
without letting at least Fern know
exactly why she was done with this place.

Poppy paces across the cabin floor
it is not like her
to do this, to be so rattled.
She makes herself pause
in front of the dresser
where the photo of all of them
in the meadow
stands
but even there something feels off
itching at her brain.

She picks up the photograph
trying to identify

what about it is bothering her.
None of the girls' faces hold any surprises,
and the landscape behind them
is as it always is,
just a field of wheat,
bending limber under a breeze,
the sky a perfect clear slate
from which evening light pours down.
It's the dresses, perhaps
something about one of them
that's gently knocking against
the wall of her skull.
I'll remember later, she thinks. It'll come to me.

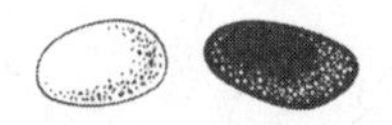

THE CAT IS AN INTERESTING DEVELOPMENT.
We've never had a pet here.
There are the cows,
and we briefly had chickens
until a fox decimated them.
But never a pet.

There once had been a dog
a red-coated stray,
with drooping ears and uneasy brown eyes.
It had come up to the campfire,
lured by the smell of roasting meat,
and then lingered.

Zachary had called it a nuisance,
said it should be yelled at,
discouraged from staying.
Hamish had flushed and shook his head
too upset for words.
Joseph had taken his side
said it was a living creature
one that had a right to be here

as long as it did not steal from us
or cause us harm.

Some of us had imagined ourselves
slowly winning it over,
until it would trot alongside us
through the orchard
and lay its head on our laps
when we sat down to eat our lunch.
Others imagined it as a guard dog,
fiercely loyal, standing outside our cabin
barking to the high heavens
should someone approach in the night.

It had stayed for a week, maybe ten days,
then it disappeared into the woods again
and we couldn't help but feel
like it had abandoned us,
found us lacking.
So as we watch the cat pace our room
settle itself amid our things
we steel ourselves
not to get too attached.

Laurel

IN FRONT OF LAUREL SITS A PLATE
of thickly sliced toast with raspberry jam.
She loves toast, loves raspberry jam,
but she is so distracted
she can barely taste it.

In part this is due to Rose.
Ever since Rose disappeared
Laurel has felt strange, off—
she is used to being in control
not accustomed to misplacing things,
and somehow she feels that's what happened
that she's left Rose in a closet
or swept her underneath the bed
and if she retraced her steps
looked in the right place,
then she'd find Rose.

But today there's also something else at play
in her distraction.

For today is the day of blessings,
their monthly opportunity to speak with Joseph.

She has been practicing
how to calmly ask him
what she can do to be better, more deserving.
Because last time
he'd put his hand under her chin
said he'd invite her to the next prayer circle,
that she was ready.
She doesn't know how she messed up,
but obviously she did.
Because otherwise a slip of paper with her name,
a date and a time
would have appeared.

After breakfast, they all form a long line
that snakes around and around.
She stands behind Fern and soon
Fern is up, speaking with Joseph.

After an infinite wait,
Fern moves along,
her forehead marked by a white dot
holding a many-petaled flower in her hand
looking like an entirely different person,
impossibly young and sweet.

Joseph looks at Laurel and smiles,
beckoning her forward
only tenderness in his clear blue eyes,
and she suddenly feels hopeful
it was a simple misunderstanding.

He reaches into the pot of white ointment,
she stands perfectly still
as he paints a single dot
on her forehead with his finger.

Do you have any questions
for me? he asks. *Any news*
you wish to share?

She takes a long deep breath.
I wanted to ask about the prayer meeting.
She hopes he'll take it from there
but he simply waits for her to finish.
Last week? she says, her voice turning
what was meant to be a statement into a question.

She suddenly feels terribly young and unsure,
like she is asking for too much,
even though it should have already been given.
Last month, you said...you said that I was ready.
That you'd invite me.
He is looking at her like she is a stranger,
like she is speaking in tongues.

Maybe you forgot? she says,
her voice taking on a pitch high and ridged.
Something dark and angry swirls in Joseph's face.

I forget nothing. I thought you were ready.
But your actions indicated you were not.

She flinches, his words hitting her as hard
as the back of his hand could.
The shock reminds her
of how one night
she'd reluctantly broken curfew
after realizing she'd forgotten
to turn off the kiln.
I'm sorry, she says. *I was worried about the kiln.*

But that is no excuse, is it?

She shakes her head, ashamed.
His face softens.

Look, you are young, he says.
You will do better.

He reaches out to touch her shoulder
and she thinks this signals a change of heart,
until she realizes he is gently pushing her away.

Ivy

Ivy had been behind Laurel in line,
had heard Joseph's uncharacteristic spike of anger,
had seen the devastation in Laurel's face
as she turned to go.
Usually, Ivy doesn't interfere
it is not her way to entangle herself
by caring too much.
Usually, at most,
she'd send someone else after Laurel
such as Poppy, Laurel's confidant,
or kind, dreamy Violet.

Yet even as Ivy told herself
she wasn't going to say anything,
that she wasn't going anywhere in particular,
she finds herself going to the riverbank
and when she sees Laurel there,
she pretends to herself this is a coincidence.

She flings her body down
so it forms a lazy C around Laurel,
props her head up on her elbow
and glances at Laurel through
long, fluttering eyelashes.
Oh, she says. *I didn't see you there.*

Laurel smiles weakly, her eyes puffy and red,
her cheeks damp.

I messed up, she says, with a hitch
in her voice.
A few weeks back, I broke a rule.
I don't know what I was thinking.

That's regrettable, of course, Ivy says,
trying to sound patient and kind,
but I'm sure you're still one of his favorites.
If he'd been truly that upset
he wouldn't have waited until now
to admonish you.

Despite Ivy's efforts, Laurel seems to hear
the slight edge of impatience in Ivy's voice,
because she looks at Ivy, appraisingly.

You act like you don't care if you are
liked by Joseph. Do you?

Her instinct is that she doesn't,
but that's not true

she simply doesn't court his affections, his trust
like Laurel.

Yes, but I also know my particular charms
don't work on him
so it does me no good
to try for something I'll never get.

She wonders if Laurel will take that as an
implied criticism,
so it's a relief when Laurel laughs.

You're probably the smartest one of
all of us, then. She pauses.
What do you think happened
to Rose?

I don't know. Perhaps the rough weather
led her to ask someone else for the ride.

Someone at Havenwood, you mean?
Do you think someone would do
that if she asked? If you did?

The shock in Laurel's voice
makes Ivy want to take it back
to say she doesn't believe that possible.
Yet she's seen things in the eyes
of the boys, the men,
even some of the girls and women
that make those words feel hollow

make her think that a request
asked the right way,
delivered into the right ear
could get her anyplace she wanted to go.
And Rose
—with that face
—with that body
could have easily done the same.
So, reluctantly,
she nods.

Daisy

Daisy had forgotten to follow through
on replenishing the clinic's supplies
leading Clara to remind her
the yarrow was low
and to comment, more sharply than usual
that she'd had to go out to the garden herself
to replenish the sage.

Luckily, this is one of those fortunate days
when the floor of the woods
acts like a pantry, a pharmacy,
and everything that Daisy wants
appears as if summoned.
And the white noise of wind
gently whipping around her
cocoons her as if she is the only one
for miles
the only one left in the world.

It is only when she starts making her way back
her bag sufficiently filled
when she realizes how untrue this is
that someone, Zachary,
is sitting against a tree trunk
only a few yards away.
He has his back to her,
his neck and shoulders tense,
not yet aware of her presence.
Zachary is usually at the center of things
with others attending to his actions and thoughts
so she assumes she has stumbled
into a small hunting party
with others nearby.
Yet when she looks around
she finds
they appear to be the only two
in the woods.

In the far distance
a tractor roars to life
she instinctively turns toward it
and when she turns back around
Zachary is looking at her
eyebrows raised
expression hard.
In his lap

there is not the rifle she expected
but a length of braided leather.

What are you doing out here?
he asks, his voice rough.
You should be helping out back at
the compound.

I've been foraging for the clinic, she says,
attempting for assertiveness yet
her voice comes out high and young
turning it almost into a question.

He glances at her bag
then shakes his head,
like he doesn't believe
a word she says.

Go on back now. This isn't a place
you should linger.

Hot words rise inside of her
and then she remembers he is no longer a peer
he is a man, he is a protégé of Joseph
one with a shimmer of barely restrained violence
behind his eyes.
Her words deflate, punctured by a prick of fear
and, to her great shame,
she does exactly as she's been told.

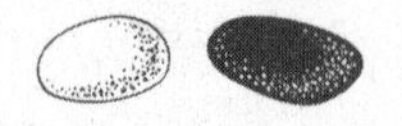

VIOLET WAKES UP BLEEDING,
and within a few hours
the rest of our bodies follow suit.
The cabin smells of iron
our nerves are on edge,
our hormones swinging wide.

When we go to the infirmary to pick up supplies,
we learn the elders failed to stock up
leaving us now very low.
When one of the male elders suggests surely
we can make do with ripped-up and wadded cotton,
we narrow our eyes in response
and a sound rises from our throats
that causes him to take a step back
and prompts Sarah to intervene,
to decree that the next day a special trip
will be made.

When we return to the cabin
we search to see if we can find a hidden cache.
Each month, we divide what we are given
equally among us.

While unused ones ought to be returned
to the communal supply,
sometimes that does not happen.

We scour the bathroom, the bedroom—
going through the wardrobe,
vexing the cat with our flurry of movement.
We go through all our drawers—
but at first we leave Rose's drawer alone,
until Daisy suddenly rebels
and yanks it wide open
—her slim wrist jerking the handle so forcefully
we expect it to come off in her hand.

We watch as she pushes aside socks, underwear
as an expression of triumph crosses her face
then fades, replaced by bewilderment.

We erase the space between us and her,
crowding around, peering into the drawer:
littered with pristine pads—dozens of them.
Two months' worth? Three? Poppy says,
gazing out at the rest of us for confirmation.
I miss mine sometimes, Daisy says quietly.
Yes, but she was always regular, Fern says quietly.
She sometimes even needed extra.

And she'd gotten sensitive about smells recently, Willow says.
She had me let out a dress, Poppy adds.
I heard her vomit in the morning a few times,
Violet says softly.

All these things add up
to a clear question that
we should have asked.
Except it never occurred to any of us
that she might have crossed that line.

Perhaps these words come far
too late, perhaps I mean nothing
to you now, but please know
my heart is broken over what I
did, over who I was. That I was
broken.

The obvious question is, am I
fixed now? Can I finally be what
you needed me to be?

I want to say yes, but that's not
entirely true—once shattered
there will always be cracks.

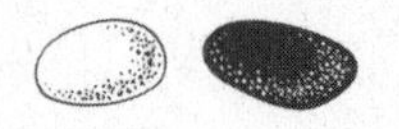

We cast our minds back,
looking for some discarded fragment:
Rose coming in late, leaving early.
Rose disheveled, avoiding our gaze.

We don't remember anything
yet three months ago, or almost,
was summer solstice
the one time each year when things loosen.
We splintered on solstice
some resolutely ignoring the revelry outside
others enjoying the sensation
of being less tethered to one another,
to ourselves than usual.
It was a night when a flushed face and crumpled clothes
could go unnoticed, uncommented on.

No one else has left, have they? Daisy asks.
She couldn't have gone to find him, to let him know?
To be with him even?
We think, throwing our minds back.
Michael left two months ago, Poppy says,
wincing as she says his name

as if the mere mention of it
might summon him back.
But I can't imagine . . .
She trails off with an apologetic shrug.
We nod, concurring with her assessment.
In addition to being a traitor,
one who'd held a position of trust
serving as Joseph's personal accountant
before absconding with a suitcase of cash
Michael was balding
small eyed and overly pink
unappealing and unintimidating.
Rose would not have gone to find him,
nor would she have hesitated to tell us
if he'd hurt her.
No one else has left though, Violet says.
Not in the months before or after.
We nod, acknowledging the truth of that.
Acknowledging
that whoever is the father,
he is still here.

Fern

FERN THINKS ABOUT WHO ROSE
would have chosen to lie with
on solstice.
For her instinct is that Rose was the selector,
not the selected.

There are girls with whom Fern
has more superficial affinities
yet despite their obvious differences—
her love of quiet, Rose's proclivity for noise—
she'd always believed she and Rose to be
parallel versions of each other.

And when boys and men emerged
half-naked from the river
in the high heat of summer
the same ones who caused a flush in her cheeks
caused a similar effect in Rose.

The most likely four options
she lays out in her mind
one by one
like playing cards.

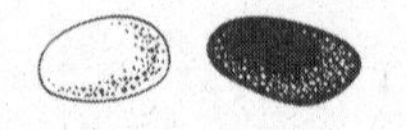

WE ARE A LITTLE SHOCKED
to learn Fern has such well-developed
thoughts on the matter
yet many of us nod
at her first suggestion: Jacob.

Jacob is in many ways
the most obvious selection,
a talented musician
beautiful and kind
whose voice could easily sway
someone not tightly tethered.

When Hamish's name is uttered
this sparks nervous giggles
ones that acknowledge both the temptation
of his perfect smile and labor-sculpted arms
and the audacity of noting the physical charms
of one of Joseph's protégés.

Zachary's name causes instead
an anxious squeeze—

he is also physically striking, yes,
and another protégé too
but even beyond these things
there is something about him
that makes us uneasy.

The last name, Peter,
is a controversial one
for he is so much older
yet he is handsome
with a low voice that thrums at a place deep within.

And Peter drinks, Violet offers. *I saw him drunk.*
Oleanna lets out a low hiss
and our eyebrows collectively rise
and then rise higher still
when Violet admits
she let it go unreported.
Laurel looks like she is about to rebuke Violet
when Ivy speaks up.
He'd probably only have gotten a warning anyway.
Both because of how he lost his family
and his friendship with Joseph.

We don't like this idea
of Joseph playing favorites

making exceptions
which isn't necessarily the same
as thinking Ivy is wrong.

I'll develop the film from the camera, Fern says,
and look through her older negatives.
Whoever he was,
she might have taken a photo of him
or of the two of them together.
I can help, Oleanna offers.
I've wanted to learn how anyway.
We appreciate Fern's suggestion
yet we are not hopeful—
Rose was never very inclined
to take photos of people.

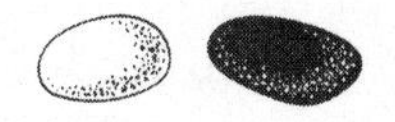

When the bell sounds
we are surprised
but we know what to do.
Those of us in the cabin
grab our designated supply bags—
filled with flashlights, batteries, and first-aid kits—
those of us outside
drop our work, take nothing with us.
An uninvited visitor
has again breached the gates.

We go into the main hall, where everyone has gathered.
One day the underground shelter will hold us all,
but there is still work on it to be done.
There are already men handing out guns
when the first of us reaches the hall.
We do not receive guns
our role is to secure the windows
to lower the heavy metal shutters
while the children light candles.

It is possible that some of us
sneak a peek through the shutters

that we briefly glimpse
the same intruder
who came a month or two earlier—
a woman with a resemblance to someone
that we can almost but not quite place.
But if we look, if we notice anything,
we do not admit it
either to ourselves
or to one another.

We do all hear the muffled sound of an exchange
the deep angry voice of an elder
a higher voice—
the intruder's surely—
angry, pleading.

A third voice enters,
calm, centered:
Sarah.

The intruder yells out, a name perhaps—
once, twice.
We strain to catch the word
yet when we later compare notes
we each heard a different one formed.
The third time is fainter, moving away
—being moved away.

We wait
it feels
like a very long time
before the all-clear is given.

Before we disperse
Sarah tells us
it was a rejected potential
an addict
who did not make it
through the screening process
who wanted the beauty of this place
without the required sacrifices.

It is a familiar narrative
we must be careful
about who we take in.

Yet
this time
some of us privately question
whether Sarah is giving us something
easy
rather than something that is true.

Oleanna

IN THE DARKROOM, THE RED LIGHT
makes the cold air almost
feel warm, soft—
like a fire providing just enough illumination
to navigate the room.
Oleanna stares around the space,
taking in the strings with clips
that stretch from wall to wall.
She is not sure yet
if she finds the darkness comforting or unnerving
if she likes being in the realm of images
instead of that of letters.
Fern on the other hand
seems completely at ease here,
relaxed and unfurled
even taller, as if she is finally fully upright
having shed an undetected hunch.

Oleanna reaches out to touch the edge
of one of the hanging photographs.

The photo is of the sky
seen through the small window
at the top of the barn.
Another is a close-up of hay
shot from a low angle
so low that Rose might have
needed to lower herself to the ground
to take it
smudging her arms
mussing her hair
turning her dark hair into
a nest fit for birds.

In the background
Oleanna barely registers as
Fern talks quietly as she prepares
the chemicals
to fix the film.
It comes as a shock
when Fern turns off the light
to wind the film
into a canister.

When Fern eventually
pulls the film out of the reel
a small frown of disappointment

bends her face and then she beckons Oleanna
to bear witness.

Even in negative form,
the images are clearly all flowers
and close-ups of trees and stumps—
no figures or faces.
The only photos that document
a living creature
are the ones of the cat
Fern took to finish the roll.

Oleanna closes her eyes
and tries to conjure up Rose
in a very different place,
in a city.
Rose on a sidewalk,
looking up at tall buildings,
marveling at their height,
passed by a blur of cars.
When she tries to add people to it,
her mind rebels.
All she sees is Rose,
walking alone.

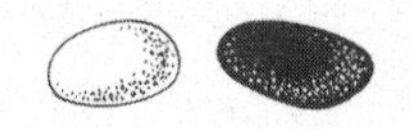

WITH THE DARKROOM
yielding no answers
more direct action is needed
so we decide someone should ask Jacob
—gently, unobtrusively—
about Rose.

He is, we feel, the safest target
with the advantages of being
neither an elder nor a protected potential successor
and while a probable choice in his own right,
he's also close enough
—physically, personally—
to Hamish and Zachary
that he might know—or at least suspect—
if it were instead one of them.

In terms of who should approach him
we indicate
as tactfully as we can
that it would be least out of character
for Ivy to start such a conversation
and that her beauty and silver-quick charm

might entice him into
letting down his guard.

We cannot tell
exactly
if Ivy is pleased or offended
by this suggestion
we only know that
she agrees.

Ivy

It is a well-known fact
that Jacob loves to swim
that he continues to go to the river at dawn
long past when others
deem the water too cool.

So, Ivy forces herself to wake early
her eyes still clouded with sleep
as she leaves,
a towel wrapped around her shoulders.

She walks quickly through the woods
a girl on a mission
yet as she approaches the river
for a brief moment she indulges herself
in the idea of finding Jacob emerging
from the water
slick and wet.

Fortunately or not
her timing is off
and when she arrives
he's already out of the river
pulling back on his shirt.

She makes sure that he's seen her
and then feigns surprise:
I'm sorry, I didn't think anyone was here,
she says. *Should I go?*

No, please, he says. *I was getting*
ready to leave.
Then he pauses, curious.
Are you here to swim?

More like float, she says.
I'm not a strong swimmer like you.
The compliment provokes a flush on his neck
so she decides to double down,
letting a look of guilty horror cross her face
like a shy girl, accidentally brazen.
Not that I've watched you swim.

It's not a crime if you did,
he says gallantly, the color on his
neck deepening.
It's not my river.

No, I couldn't do that. Not to Rose.
She flies her hands to her mouth

as if she's again said too much.
Jacob's brow furrows
with what seems like true confusion.

Rose? Your friend?
Why would she mind?

There's a rumor she was seen with a boy.
In an . . . intimate situation.
Your name was mentioned.

That didn't happen.
Not with me anyway.

They described the boy as young, tall—
she pauses, pretends to think
—perhaps it was Hamish? Or *Zachary?*

At that second name
Jacob's eyes go large
and his hand jerks up in a warning.
You shouldn't go around
suggesting that.
Especially not about Zachary.

Because it's not true? Or *because it is?*

Because he wouldn't like it.

His tone makes her think
there's more to Zachary's anger than she knows
and she'd thought she knew plenty.
She opens her mouth to ask
him to expand
but he shakes his head.

I don't know who Rose was seen
with, he says gently, *and if I happen*
to learn, I'll do my best to forget it.
I'd strongly recommend you do
the same.

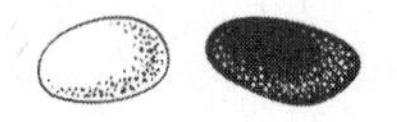

We are not sure
what to do with what Jacob said.
It is a warning, it seems,
but from someone
who truly seems to mean us no harm.
And yet Rose is still missing,
and the father of her child
is still here.

We feel disoriented,
unsure of our feelings about it all.

If we'd been asked
months before
if we would miss Rose
should she suddenly disappear
we'd have immediately,
automatically
said yes.

Yet if we'd been asked why
there might have been a pause
as we considered

how quiet it could be without her
how nice it might be not to hear exactly
what someone thought of us.

We would not have known
how much we'd miss her stories
her crackling laugh
not yet recognized the communal benefit
of her casual uttering
of unkind but often shared sentiments—
relieving us all of irritants such as
Ivy's tuneless humming
Violet's endless musings about bees.

We hadn't understood how
we'd unconsciously shaped ourselves
against Rose
how we'd been allowed
to be easy and gentle
because she was not.

And so yes, we miss her,
but also we miss
the people
the group
we were when she was here.

And we want to understand
if she is going to return
if we're going to get
to become those people
that group
again.

Daisy

THE CAT SLEEPS CURLED UP AGAINST DAISY,
its fur pressed tight to her body.
She had not expected this creature to love her,
for it to so brazenly
prefer her to the others,
as though the cat has sensed some
innate goodness in her that the others lack.

She likes this sensation, of being chosen,
likes it so much it's hard
to displace this small warm creature,
even though her bladder is almost
at the point of bursting.

She must though, so she gently pushes it off her,
earning herself a sleepy look of betrayal
before it stretches and
nestles into the warm outline
of where her body was seconds before.

She's heading toward the lodge
when she stops, surprised to see two figures
out by the hives.
She assumes, at first,
the woman in the bee suit is Violet
yet the figure is different, taller
and Violet always tends to her bees alone.

The demands of her bladder
temporarily disappear
as she watches.
The woman lifts up a frame,
lays a gloved finger gently on it
and waits.
Then she closes the hive with her other hand,
and then steps toward the man,
who rolls up his sleeve, exposing his forearm,
which he holds out like an offering.
The woman gently brushes her glove
against his exposed skin,
as if depositing something onto it
and then makes a fast, slapping motion.
The man flinches, slightly.
They do this again, and again
before the man unrolls his sleeve,
and buttons it at the wrist.

When he turns in Daisy's direction
she moves quickly out of view
but first
with a start
she recognizes his face.

Willow

DAISY IS NOT MUCH OF A READER
so Willow is surprised to see her
enter the library.
I don't think I've ever seen you
in here before, Willow says.
While this is both true
and gently said
it prompts a flush to rise on Daisy's cheeks
and Willow wishes she could retract the remark.
Daisy has, she knows,
sometimes presented all too easy
a target.
Can I help you find something? Willow offers.

I'm looking for something on flora
and fauna used for medicinal
purposes, Daisy says.

Willow rises.
Over here are the ones on natural medicines,
she says, pointing.
What are you looking for, exactly?

I saw something…odd, and we keep running out of sage. I'm trying to understand why.

As answers go
this is hardly expansive
yet Daisy seems unwilling to provide additional details.
So Willow watches as Daisy takes down
a reference text on natural medicines
and looks up sage
then—to Willow's surprise—
apitherapy—
the use of bee products
honey, pollen, venom
to deal with ailments.
Who's using sage and honey? Willow asks.
When Daisy looks up,
there is a troubled expression on her face,
as if the answers on the page
cause her pain.

It's venom, not honey, Daisy says quietly and then stops. *Nobody. I was just curious.*

Daisy is, Willow thinks,
a poor liar
but she nods, pretending to believe her
to avoid upsetting her further.

Poppy

EARLIER, SARAH HAD APPROACHED POPPY
about making Helen a dress.
It would be so nice, Sarah said,
for Helen to have something
in time for her initiation ceremony.
Technically, it was asked as a request
but like all requests from Sarah
it was not one to be easily turned down.

While Poppy had been quietly irritated
at having to put aside her planned projects
Helen is, Poppy must admit,
a much better model than many.
Even her child is well behaved,
quietly lying on a blanket in the corner,
fascinated by an old wooden spool.
He's so good, Poppy says. *So easy.*

It's not going to last, Helen says.
He's started crawling. Soon, he'll be
unstoppable.

Poppy smiles, motions for Helen to raise her arm.
So, how are you finding Havenwood?

Good. I mean, it's beautiful here.
I've been hopeless in the kitchen,
but I'm interested in architecture
so they're going to have me help
with the infirmary addition.
Which is wonderful.

She's smiling, earnest,
yet there's also a hesitation in her voice,
as if she's holding something back.
It's an adjustment being here, Poppy says lightly.
It's understandable if you miss
parts of the outside world.

It's not that. It's more—
she pauses, and glances toward the
door, as if reassuring herself that
it is indeed shut.
I want to feel this intense
connection
you all have with Joseph
but he's met me three times now,
and it still seems like he barely even
recognizes me.

Of course he does, Poppy says.
He's just busy, has a lot on his mind.

Yes, of course. I just... I think I was hoping for a clear sign, you know? That coming here was the right choice.

Helen looks apologetic,
yet Poppy is angered by this needy woman
who so casually demands Havenwood
provide her with immediate validation.
And the pin in Poppy's hand briefly twitches
as if wishing to firmly push itself
into Helen's skin.

Fern

FERN'S MORNING HAS PROVED
less than ideal.
Her preferred knife
is still missing from the block
and she's had to spend valuable minutes
clearing the counter of an insomniac's debris—
a cutting board, a knife slick with peanut butter.
The culprit, Fern suspects, is Oleanna
known for her bouts of insomnia
and early morning snacking.

Fern turns at the sound of footsteps
and is surprised
to find Joseph there
looking around the kitchen
his face holding the particular searching gaze
she's seen many times before
on many different faces.
Coffee? she hazards.
He finds her face and smiles.

I am but an open book, I see.
For anyone else, she would merely
gesture toward the French press.
For him though, she does not dream
of doing anything other than what she does,
which is to proceed to make it for him.
Thank you, he says. *I usually try to*
stick to tea, but this morning I woke
up thinking of coffee.
Would you like it with milk? Sugar?
Yes. Milk, and a teaspoon of sugar,
please.
How about cinnamon? she asks, feeling bold.
Not everyone likes it, but I think it's a nice
addition.
Certainly, he says, with a faint
smile. *I'll try anything once.*
She has never focused on coffee
like this before
never been so anxious to get it right.
She mixes the cinnamon in with the milk
just enough to make itself known
and then stirs the mixture into the coffee.

When she hands him the cup
he sips from it then smiles.

That's lovely, he says.
So clever of you to think to add
that in.

She ducks her head in response
and inside, she glows.

Ivy

There's a particularly big pile
of mail today
and Ivy feels like she has
been sorting it for endless hours.
Oleanna, of course,
has not complained
dutifully takes her notes
writing down "Grandmother dying"
with the same impassive expression
as she writes "Favorite food: tomato soup."
Another girl Ivy might tease about her intensity
but Oleanna has very thin skin
too often pricked by Rose
and she might retaliate with a brusque comment
about Ivy's leisurely approach
to mail sortage.

And today Ivy is indeed slow
distracted by a thought lodged in her mind

like a stubborn thorn:
how Rose had not told anyone,
not even Fern—
what had happened.
If Ivy ever transgressed that way,
done what she'd imagined more than once—
slipping off her dress, joining Jacob in the river—
she would likely not tell anyone
yet it stings that she did not even
have an obvious person to tell.
That thought leaves a bruise
makes her wonder if
despite rarely being actually alone
she is perhaps lonely.

She forces herself to concentrate on the mail
an electricity bill
which she flags with a scrap of red tape
a few letters addressed to Joseph—
two from a women's prison,
where he once gave a lecture—
and a series of advertisements,
a clothing catalog.

She's almost at the bottom of the pile
when she comes across

a plain white envelope
with a little plastic window.
It is utterly unremarkable other than the name
to which it is addressed:
Rose.

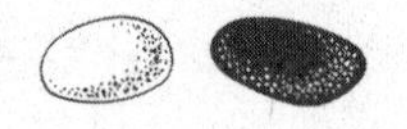

Ivy takes a letter from
her pocket
and lays it out on the bed.
We can tell that she and Oleanna
have both already read it,
so we wait for one of them to explain,
but they both stay quiet.
Poppy finally picks it up,
and we watch as she reads it.

She hands it to Daisy,
and it travels around all of us in this way.
The letter is from a clinic
a bill for a missed appointment,
one set for the day she disappeared.
We do not know what the appointment was for
whether it means she wanted to keep the baby
or if she very much did not.

Daisy

THERE IS A SINGLE PHONE IN THE COMPOUND,
a landline, located in the hall by Joseph's bedroom,
hung high on the wall
intended only for emergencies.
None of them have ever used it.

Daisy was pleased the others nominated her
to call the clinic
and she can see Poppy and Fern standing watch
ready to distract anyone
who might attempt to venture down the hall.
Still, she is so well trained not to touch this phone,
not to consider its existence,
part of her believes its plastic will sear her skin,
branding her with a telltale burn
marking her disobedience.

She does not have the letter in her hand
but the number is bright in her mind.

The phone is answered after three rings

This is Southland Wellness Clinic.

The voice is female, pleasant and firm
that of someone used to enforcing boundaries
who also has tissues in their office.
Hello.
Daisy's voice shakes.
She flicks herself on the wrist once, hard,
trying to get herself under control.
My name is Rose.
I had an appointment but I missed it.
She takes a breath, gearing herself up to plow ahead,
to try and get answers,
but the woman's softened voice
comes on the line again.

Ah, she says. *Are you wanting to reschedule?*

Yes. Maybe.

You can take more time if you need to think it through or put together the money.
Once the first trimester ends though, termination gets more complicated.

Termination.
There is a stretch of silence before she realizes
the woman is waiting for her to respond.

I understand, Daisy says.
She tries to say it like she believes
Rose might have,
when confronted with how a lack of a decision
could soon be a decision of its own.
But her voice wavers
where Rose's would have stayed steady
and she quickly hangs up the phone.

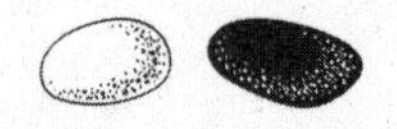

AFTER DAISY TELLS US ABOUT THE CALL,
we turn the information around, dissect it.
Rose did not want to keep the child.
She made an appointment,
she was on her way there
but she did not make it.

The phone has answered only one question,
about Rose's original intention for the ride,
for the appointment.
Perhaps Madison
has some other answers.

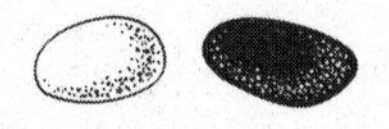

Last time, we went all together
and that was too much, we think.
This time three of us go:
Poppy, Violet, and Daisy.
One person could go alone, yet we pick three.
We don't talk about why that is
about whether we want Madison
to be outnumbered,
or whether we suspect
that one person alone might not bring back
the full truth.

We're over the fence and
only halfway across the field
before Madison comes out of the house and
starts walking across the field toward us.

She looks neither pleased nor surprised to see us
her hands stay down by her sides
as she strides through the grass
her face holding a look of weary inevitability.
She knows, we know, this is not a social call.

Is she still missing? she asks.

Yes, Poppy says.
And we've learned about the baby.
What did she tell you about it?

Only that it was consensual.

Daisy speaks up.
She didn't say anything about the father?

No. Madison pauses, a frown
forming on her face.
Look, it's been over a week.
Shouldn't you have brought in
the police?
Are the adults trying to keep
this a secret?

No. We told them she was hurt, staying in bed—
Violet starts, and then she pauses,
looking to the other two of us for confirmation
that an adult has indeed
asked about Rose.
We each wait, expecting someone to say yes,
that they'd been asked about her
that they'd used our prepared line.
But no one does.

Madison watches as we falter,
unable to successfully answer
her simple question.

You know, you don't have to stay
there, she says softly.
I could help you leave.

We do not doubt her intentions
or sincerity
yet we are quietly angered
by her misinterpretation of our lives
by her belief that our world
might require her intervention
that leaving it might be anything other
than a devastating loss.

Finally Daisy speaks up,
if only to close out the conversation.
We don't need your help, Daisy says.
But thank you for helping Rose.

I didn't though. I never gave her
that ride.

No, but you must have given her
the information about the clinic,
maybe money too.

No, I didn't. She said she had the
money and she'd already scheduled
the appointment.
All she asked for was a ride.

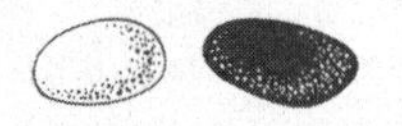

When we all come together
we learn the strange truth:
that since the child asked us about Rose
no one else has asked any of us
to account for Rose's whereabouts.

We've been acting like
she has been gone only but a day or two
and that we fully expect her to return any moment
to waltz right back in
with a glorious, overwrought story
of her escapades in the wider world
and perhaps even
sincere gratitude and relief
for keeping her absence a secret.

Yet Madison is right, we realize,
it has been too long now
much longer than we'd expected
and Rose is not a lightweight presence.
While it is understandable that some might
not wish to admit they'd noticed the absence
of such a very pretty girl

surely someone other than a child
should have asked
where she is.
We keep to ourselves
yes, more than many
and no, others don't always come to us
don't inquire about us like they might others
but surely, at least one of the adults
should have asked.

There is also the quandary that
—like all of us—
Rose had no money of her own
and without assistance
she would not have known
where to call
what number to dial.

We do not like the conclusion
to which this leads us:
That someone had to have helped her.
Someone at Havenwood.

My Dear One,

I promised myself I wouldn't do this. That I would respect your decision if you didn't write back, and leave you be.

Yet here I am, doing the exact opposite. I have no real excuse; all I can say is that you are all I think about these days.

You haunt me, yet when I try to picture your face, all I can see is my own.

Willow

WHEN VIOLET SUGGESTS THAT SHE AND WILLOW
go on a walk,
Willow almost stutters in her eagerness
to say yes.
She wants to have time alone with Violet,
yes, of course,
but she also needs to get out of the cabin
which feels too small,
too populated.

Today the tension between the two of them
is less a sparkling bolt
and more of a low thrum, a pulsation.
This too is a reprieve of sorts—
the intense bodily pleasure Violet gives her
is sometimes shaded by an anxious guilt
even though it has been months now
and—as far as she can tell—
no repercussions have come,
not to her or to anyone else.

You've been quiet, Willow says.
What are you thinking about?

I've been thinking about Rose,
her being pregnant.
About what it would be like
to have that as a choice.

Is it a choice you want?

No.

Violet says it quickly, so quickly
it seems more like a reflex
than a response.

I've just been thinking about it, is all.
What it would feel like to have
something of my own.

Willow stares at Violet's perfect, earnest face
and though it is still daylight,
she does not scan the fields
before she puts her hand on Violet's cheek.

I'm yours, Willow says quietly.
I belong to you.

Violet kisses her
once
twice
three

times
but she does not say it back.
And this leaves Willow off-balance
unsure
whether these kisses
were intended as an affirmation
or a distraction.

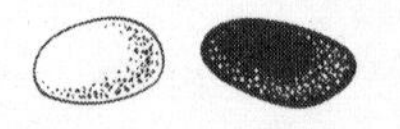

In the middle of the night
there's a scream,
impossibly loud,
impossibly wild.
We jolt up
sure that a feral beast
has entered the cabin,
and we look frantically around the dark
for the source of the sound.

It takes a while
before we realize it is Oleanna
who is screaming,
her eyes moving rapidly underneath
her closed eyelids,
her body flailing under the sheet.

We stroke her hair, call out her name,
trying to wake her,
trying to get the screams to stop
telling her that it's okay
that she's with us
but she has a hard time

surfacing
and we wonder—
not for the first time—
if she remembers more than she admits
about the accident that claimed her parents
when she was so young
if her dream involves
the high shriek of brakes
the shattering of glass
the rank scent of the drunk culprit
who walked away unscathed.

After we get Oleanna awake
we brace ourselves to hear running footsteps,
fists pounding at the door,
raised voices asking if we are okay.
We are fine, we prepare ourselves to say—
it was only a nightmare.
Yet no one comes, not fast, not slow
and so these words remain unused on our tongues.

And our return to sleep is slowed
by the knowledge
that we are even more alone here
than we'd realized.

Daisy

IT'S LAUNDRY DAY
and Daisy is collecting the baskets
of dirty clothes
from outside of the lodge
and depositing them
into the wheeled hamper.

The older boys' basket
is not outside, where it should be.
Its absence should be their problem,
not hers,
but it won't play out that way.
Reluctantly, she abandons the hamper
and goes inside.

The boys' area smells dank and musty,
soaked through with sweat.
The basket is on the other side of the room,
socks and underwear flopping down its sides.

She notices that on two of the beds
lie little slips of paper.
One has Hamish's name on it
the other Zachary's
and both bear the same time—
midnight a few days from now—
written in pencil in a long, flowing scrawl.
Other than the names
they are identical to the notes
Oleanna receives
although hers are left outside the cabin,
weighed down with a small rock.

It's funny they choose pencil for this,
she thinks, not ink
and her mind turns to
Zachary sitting under that tree
with his length of leather
telling her to get gone.
And she wonders what would happen
if someone else showed up instead
someone more worthy
someone who'd long hoped
for an invitation.
If that person would get turned away
or if, perhaps,

they would simply be accepted without question
if the writer might not even recognize
that a change had been made.

For a moment
she is unsure of whether she wants
to know the answer
to test her evolving theory
but then her fingers drift toward Zachary's slip of paper,
and she lightly scoops it
into the palm of her hand.

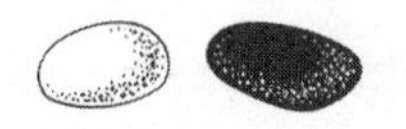

We are so happy for Laurel
because after dinner there it was,
that little slip of paper
with her name on it
under the rock
right along with Oleanna's.

Laurel is in the prayer circle now,
just as she'd hoped to be
for so long.

I'm never going to mess with curfew again,
she says, laughing a little.

We all laugh with her
even though many of us don't know
what she's talking about
because we all do that sometimes
forget we don't share all our thoughts.

Besides, it's true we must respect curfew
even if it's been imposed more often recently
often announced by Sarah or Joseph

on short notice.
We've heard others complain about it,
quietly but not so quietly that we can't hear them,
but that is not something we'd do.
By keeping Rose's absence a secret
we are skating on thin ice
and we have no interest
in seeing it break.

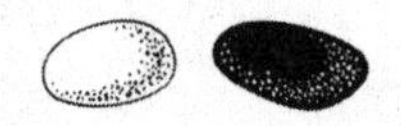

THIS MORNING
a fog lies so heavy and low
the tops of the apple trees are invisible
the trunks disintegrating into the white gray.
We all wear sweaters,
with long-sleeve shirts underneath.

In the hall
there is a long stretch of silence after we are all seated.
When Joseph makes his way to the podium,
he moves slowly
like he is walking underwater
each step made only by a great effort of will.
He stands with both hands stretched out
across the podium,
his head heavy on his neck.

It gives me great sorrow to tell you,
a trespass was made, he says.
That another Michael, another
betrayer, has been in our midst.

A murmur begins to swell in the room,
and he quells it with an uplifted hand.

We will pray now, and we will eat.
And then we shall gather in the
yard.

The room is so quiet
we can practically hear the blood pulse
through one another's veins,
hear the soft thud, thud, thud
of everyone's heartbeats.
Someone tried to hurt the community
someone is going to be made to pay.
We are angry.
        We are excited.
We are sickened.
        We are thrilled.

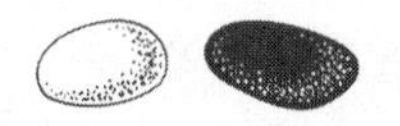

THE MAN LED TO STAND
in the center of the rock circle
is Peter.
There is a look on his face
that transforms it
from handsome to hunted
his eyes darting around the circle
a wild animal caught in a trap.

This man, Joseph tells us, *has been*
taking from the treasury, has been
imbibing alcohol.

He holds up as evidence
a silver flask,
and a pile of folded bills—
held together with a lilac rubber band.

That money isn't mine, Peter says.
I don't understand how it got into
my room.

His gravelly voice is higher than usual
and he sounds panicked, untrustworthy.
Most of us are transfixed,
watching only Peter and Joseph,

everyone else fading far into the background.
Yet some of us see Sarah,
who has a small frown on her face
like she is trying to calculate something
not finding a solid answer.

I found it myself, Joseph says.
Are you questioning my word?

Peter shakes his head, quickly, furiously.
Then, to our surprise, Sarah speaks:

And what about the alcohol?
Are you telling us that isn't yours
either?

The alcohol was mine, he admits,
after a long pause.

Sarah nods,
and takes the smallest of steps back.
A frown remains on her face,
but she says no more.

You can leave, Joseph says calmly.
If you admit to all you did.
But if you lie, or try to stay,
there will be no choices left for you.

We watch as Peter bites his lip,
unwilling to confess.
Silence is not an acceptable answer.

A man scoops up a rock,
and then another follows.
Our fingers itch even as our hearts pound.

A woman is bending down
when Peter speaks,
his eyes trained on the woman's hand,
the rock a few inches beneath her fingertips.
I admit it.
The woman pauses.

You know we need more than that,
Joseph tells him.

I admit to taking what was not mine to take,
Peter says, his voice a fraction louder.
The alcohol is mine,
and the money is also mine.
I took it.
He watches the woman's hand
move away from the rock,
and when he starts to speak again
there is a new steadiness in his voice.
Instead of focusing on our shared future
I let my past
lead me back to drink.
Instead of being content to share
in our communal wealth
I took money for my own.

Joseph strides forward
puts his hand on Peter's neck
for a moment
they both close their eyes and lean forward.

Then Joseph releases Peter,
and, eyes downcast,
Peter makes his way to his bag.
The circle opens to let him go
and soon his retreating form
is swallowed by the mist.

Poppy

Poppy is by herself
working on the hem
of Helen's dress
her hands caught up in fabric
when she finds Helen hovering
looking unsettled.
Is everything all right? Poppy asks.

Helen starts to nod, then shakes
her head. *What was that this
morning?*

I'm sorry?

Peter. The stones.

*He stole from us. Consumed alcohol.
So he was asked to leave.*

*I understand that part. But the
rocks... Would people actually have
thrown them?*

Poppy makes herself smile at Helen
be patient with her.
It's a ritual, she tells her. *A reminder that*

there are consequences for actions.
That there is no room for negotiation
after Joseph's decision is made.

A ritual?

Yes. Picking up a rock means…
She finds herself thinking of the two pebbles
she carries,
their smooth white and black surfaces.
Except that's not quite right,
and she wants to be honest,
or at least precise.
It's like seconding a motion in a meeting.
A way of confirming the decision.

So, it's not really a threat.
It's only symbolic.

A wave of tension seems to release
from Helen's body
so Poppy nods.

Well, thank goodness, Helen says
with a light, slightly nervous laugh.
You know, for a second I could
almost imagine how it would feel
to throw one. She shakes her head.
Not that I ever would, of course.

Poppy smiles. *Of course,* she echoes.

Ivy

Ivy had listened
as some of the girls speculated
that it was possible
probable even
that one mystery had been solved:
that Peter was likely
the father of Rose's child.

She had nodded, agreed even that
it was a straightforward solution:
A handsome man who did not pay attention to the rules,
a beautiful, reckless girl.

And, yes,
the practicalities could also fit:
Peter had been found with money, after all,
and as someone often tasked to make trips into town
he had easy access to a vehicle.
Rose could have made a last-minute choice
to instead have him drive her to the city

where she could have swerved again—
deciding to keep the child
and not return.

Yet while the alcohol was his
—yes, Ivy believes that part of his confession—
she can't help but think that the money was not
and her perhaps vain brain
keeps whispering that Peter never struck her
as a man repressing his instincts
to fit into Havenwood's strictures.
She'd never felt his eyes follow her form
and she does not believe they followed Rose's either.

Peter as the father is a tidy solution
yet Ivy simply cannot convince herself
that he'd ever so much as considered
lying with Rose.

Laurel

THE PRAYER CIRCLE IS HELD
in a candlelit room
where only just over a dozen
others have gathered.
Laurel has been here for three hours,
yet her body is still thrumming
from the thrill of it.

When she entered
Sarah had raised her eyebrows for a brief moment
but Joseph had simply smiled at Laurel
like all had been forgiven.
She immediately felt so
incredibly welcomed and included
and she made a mental note to reassure
earnest Daisy
who'd seemed oddly anxious
about Laurel's reception.

Now Sarah is painting the backs of her hands
with tiny, focused strokes
a gift of attention, of belonging.

She looks at Oleanna,
hoping to swap a smile with her
but Oleanna is busy painting the hands of an elder
something Laurel realizes
she too will now
soon be called to do.

Joseph has been leading a prayer
and suddenly he stops,
nodding his head to punctuate the end.
He looks around the circle, taking in each of their faces,
slowly, deliberately.
When his eyes meet hers,
the breath pauses in her lungs,
and when his gaze moves on,
Laurel is relieved and bereft in equal measure.

I know how deeply you all believe
in this place, he says quietly.
And so I rely on you more
than I can the others.

Laurel feels herself blushing,
as if his words are addressed to her alone.

This place can withstand strong
storms, yet tiny cracks can still
spread from within.
Tell me what I already know so I can
be sure you'll always put
Havenwood first.

One by one, they go around the circle
telling stories of small trespasses—
words that undermined the spirit of the community,
items hoarded rather than shared,
touches that lingered overly long.

He is so appreciative of the admissions
she is at first eager to offer something up,
not about the girls, of course,
yet she's witnessed
other small trespasses.

But then she suddenly thinks back to
the day of blessing
and Joseph's sharp rebuke
and she wonders, with a bright flare of anger,
if her own almost accidental trespass
had been revealed in this very circle
with no regard to all the work she's done

to be worthy—
all the work she's done
to cleanse herself of her mother's stain.

So when he comes to her,
she bows her head.
I'm sorry, she says.
But I have neither heard nor seen anything.
She holds her breath
shocked by her own words
but no lightning strikes
or words of disappointment follow.
Instead he simply moves on
leaving her uncertain
if she has failed his test
or passed her own.

Violet

VIOLET HOPES WILLOW
will understand
why she has been absent lately
that she will see what Violet
has made for her
and realize how Violet had felt
a mere instinctive echoing of words
—I belong to you too—
had seemed inadequate as an offering
to what Willow had given her.

She is a little worried
Willow may have interpreted
things differently
Violet forgets sometimes
how trust can be fragile.

She is guiding Willow through the meadow
toward the river

and when the grass is long enough to hide their hands,
she intertwines her fingers with Willow's.

When Willow suddenly lets go
Violet feels a shock of hurt
until she sees a tall figure
loping through the field—
Hamish.
It will only be a matter of time
before he notices them,
so Violet calls out as if she's pleased to see him.

His head jolts up, and he stops midstride
then smiles without teeth.
When he reaches them,
he looks down at his boots
smeared with layers of mud.

Perfect day for a walk, isn't it?

She and Willow both laugh.
I wish we could go straight into
crisp winter, Violet says. *Instead of*
dealing with this gray damp.

Are you feeling better? Willow asks politely.
Last time we spoke, you were feeling
poorly.

Yes, thank you. He laughs,
unexpectedly. *I ate one wrong*
thing, and was in the clinic
for three nights.
I'm just thankful I didn't miss
anything important.

Did you end up finding that book?
Willow asks him.
The red leather-bound one?

No, he says. *But I think it may have*
actually been someone's personal
copy, not from the library at all.

Violet is distracted
and at first the words themselves
don't catch.
Then they come together in her mind:
A red leather-bound book
a personal copy
one not from the library.
This is a mystery
to which she may have the answer.

Willow

THEY HAVE CHANGED COURSE
away from the river
into the woods.
I want to show you something, Violet says quietly.
Willow lets herself be led
through the trees
which push closer and closer around them,
their trunks thickening,
their leaves turning colors but not yet fallen,
letting in less and less light.
These woods didn't use to be here, she tells Violet,
attempting to drown out her own thoughts.
A long time ago, this would have been a glacier
the whole state covered with thick ice.
Woolly mammoths roamed here.
Before that, dinosaurs.
She is still rambling in this manner
when she realizes
Violet has halted
in front of a particularly large oak tree

and begun reaching into a hollow
in its trunk.
This is your spot? Willow asks.
No, Violet says. *This is Rose's.*
And then she pulls out a bag,
and removes its contents, one by one:
a tiny child-size bracelet,
a thread-worn blanket,
and a book of poetry,
leather-bound red.

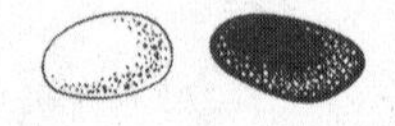

Willow and Violet share with the rest of us,
about Hamish and the book.
About what this may mean about Hamish and Rose.

Many of us are secretly relieved:
Hamish is handsome and kind—
as Joseph's protégé, the idea is shocking,
but as a boy, as a man,
he is an understandable mistake.

We should confirm it, Daisy ventures.
They could have been closer than we knew,
could have simply talked about the book.
She blushes as she says it,
looking exactly as young as we think of her as.
I'll ask him, Fern says quietly.
I think it should be me.

Fern

HAMISH IS ALONE,
on the steps of the main hall,
using a small knife to whittle a piece of wood.
Fern sits down close to him
and for a while she says nothing,
only watches as he makes slow, deliberate cuts.

It's a deer he's carving into the wood
one with antlers that extend wide
like the branches of a tree.

You slept with Rose, she says.
Simply, like the fact she believes it to be.
His knife slips
and he pauses before lowering it,
but when he answers her,
his voice is steady.

Yes, he says. *Once.*

She wants to ask him what it felt like,
being with her,
but she does not know how.
Instead, she asks:
Was it her idea or yours?
He blushes at this,
but she does not retract the question.

I don't think either of us thought of it
that way, he says. *We were talking,*
and she showed me a poem in that
book, and then . . .
He looks back at Fern.
I heard she had a bad cold—
is she still sick?

Fern blinks, disoriented—
the excuse they'd decided on
was a twisted ankle, not a cold.
Where did you hear that?

He looks sheepish. *I asked someone*
a few days ago.
I know I shouldn't have noticed
she hasn't been at the meals,
that I should put her out of my
mind entirely, but I can't help it.
I always find myself looking for her.

Fern had wondered
if he might have known,

or at least suspected,
about the baby, but nothing
in his open, guileless face
suggests that.
So, she answers him with a gentle lie
that will continue to buy Rose time.
It proved to be more of a bad flu
than a mere cold,
but she's starting to feel a bit better.

A hawk appears in the sky,
swooping down low
distracting them both
with the grace of its wing
the deep slope of its movement
toward some unlucky prey.

When she looks back at him
her mind
without her permission
takes his features and Rose's
and puts them into a small round face.

I think I fell a little in love with her
that night, he says quietly.

Did you tell her that?

No, I didn't have a chance.

We were found, asleep together.
Made to promise to never speak or
touch again.

Who found you? Who made you promise?

Sarah.

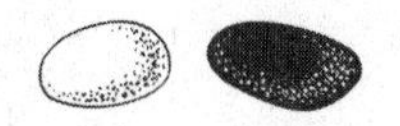

We do not want to believe
what Fern has told us.
It is too upsetting
the idea of Sarah knowing about
Rose and Hamish
and saying nothing.

Yet Sarah would have known about the clinic
and had access to money.
She could have told Rose to get a ride
from Madison,
in order to avoid involving others at Havenwood
and maintain her own distance
should things go wrong.
And when Rose did not return
Sarah could have spread the rumor
about Rose being bedbound with a cold.

So though we do not want to believe
what Fern told us, we do.
And Sarah, we agree,
owes us an explanation.

I sometimes look at the marks on my arms, my stomach, and force myself to think about all the ways I've let people down, all the wrong decisions I've made.

The way I failed you, abandoned you, was the worst betrayal of all—leaving you with nothing more than a silver circle for your tiny wrist.

You were perfect, and you should have changed everything.

What does it mean about me that you didn't?

Laurel

Laurel waits until the next day
after breakfast.
Then
with a heart that is heavy
and a shiver of nerves running through her
Laurel follows Sarah
out of the building
out toward the orchard.

There is a bench near the edge of the orchard
where Sarah alights
and with perfect posture
faces the woods.

You can sit with me, Laurel,
Sarah says, without turning.

Laurel flinches,
wanting to pretend that was not her intention
before swallowing her false claims
and obeying Sarah's suggestion
turned command.

You saw Rose and Hamish together,
she says, afraid she'll falter
if she pauses too long.
She came to you when she realized
she was pregnant.
Sarah does not immediately respond
but then she inclines her head
in a graceful half nod.

There was a conversation, yes.

But you didn't say anything to us
when she didn't come back.
You just told people that she was sick.

I assumed she'd changed her mind,
chosen to keep the child and leave.
But I also thought there was a
chance she'd change it back.

There is a strained quality
a past-tense caveat
to how she says *thought*
reminding Laurel of Sarah's flickering face,
her questions, during Peter's denouncement.
You asked Peter about the money
he allegedly stole.
Was that the money you gave Rose?

Yes. That was the only time I used
those lilac rubber bands—they break

too easily. I'd actually used two—
one must have snapped.
Why did you give her money though?
Why didn't you make her and Hamish leave?
I believed it was a one-time mistake.
That it would be kind to be discreet.
This is simple, straightforward
but also, Laurel believes, untrue.
A coupling that resulted in a pregnancy
should never have seen such leniency.
Concealing such a trespass
was an enormous risk to take on behalf
of a girl Sarah had never favored.
Laurel gambles.
It wasn't about Rose, was it?
It was Hamish that you were protecting.
No, Sarah says. *I was protecting all*
of us.
Before Laurel can respond
Sarah has risen from the bench
barely pausing to indicate
that Laurel should follow
before she starts into the woods.
Her footsteps trace a long path
that seems to exist
perfectly formed
in her mind.

They finally stop
in front of a large outcropping of rock
with a slim passage into
what seems to be a small cave.
Sarah nods toward the opening.

Joseph has two potential
successors, and two only.
If Hamish was banished, Joseph
would not pick another. Would not
believe the form Zachary's anger
takes when he thinks
no one is watching.

Laurel waits
but Sarah says nothing more.
Puzzled, Laurel angles herself
through the passage
crouching slightly until it opens up.
She finds herself standing in a small, dry space
the ground littered with small skeletons,
mostly from squirrels, rabbits,
but also foxes, fawns.
And one, she knows,
in the sick depths of her stomach
belonged to a dog
one she'd once imagined as a protector,
but that had not, in the end,
been able to protect even itself.

For around the bones of its neck
is a slim braided length of leather cord,
formed into a slipknot that had
been pulled very, very tight.

Fern

Joseph is in the kitchen again
and Fern is trying to be very calm about it.
They exchanged nods when he came in,
she made him some coffee
which he accepted with
a gracious nod and a low thank-you.

Even the act of making coffee
takes on a larger significance
when she's making it for him.

The danishes are in the oven,
their edges still yet to turn golden,
but she knows it will happen,
that she's done everything right.

Out the window, she sees Helen
talking with one of the elders
who is trying to show her

some kind of blueprint.
Helen's child is in her arms,
but he's getting fractious,
increasingly red in the face,
plump limbs pinwheeling.
Helen pulls a face of apology,
sheds her coat and makes a nest of it
on the ground,
and lays the child down on it.

Fern looks back down at her pastry
considering what she will fill it with.
Mushrooms in herbed gravy would go well
though Ivy would disagree
because Ivy hates mushrooms,
yet Ivy is wrong, Fern is certain of that.
She could make Ivy like mushrooms.

When she glances up from the counter
Helen and the elder are still there
Helen looking closely at the blueprint
her coat nest at her feet.
Fern starts to return to her pastry
then realizes the child is no longer on the coat.
She cranes toward the window
to give herself a wider view

and finds the child crawling
surprisingly quick
across the yellowing grass.
It is heading right toward
the beehives.

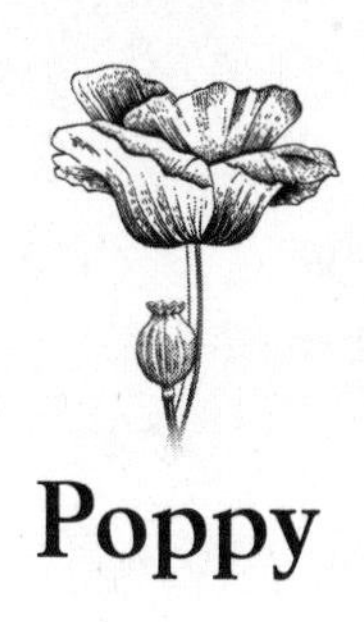

Poppy

Poppy is hauling boxes of apples
out of the orchard
when she looks up and sees
the kitchen window
framing Fern's panicked face.

Poppy follows Fern's gaze
and through the trees
she sees the outline of the child
its chubby fingers
reaching toward a hive.

She opens her mouth,
but the raw, crackling scream
that breaks the air
is not hers, but Helen's.

And for what feels like enough time to reset
every wrong decision ever made,
the child seems to pause.

But then
with a force beyond what
it should be able to summon
it slams its hand
against the hive.

Poppy freezes, arm outstretched,
until her head is twisted
by peripheral movement—
Joseph running.
He is followed by Helen,
but he has a long lead
and his limbs are almost pure blur.

A whirring noise begins
and a cloud of bees emerges
and the child raises its eyes
with wonder not yet curdled into fear.

The cloud is darkening
forming an inevitable decision
yet Joseph does not slow for a second
even as—in almost a single motion—
he swoops his arm down
to gather the child to his chest
and pulls his shirt over his head
to cover the child.

A swarm follows him
like angry smoke
covering his eyes,
his face, his back,
yet he staggers forward
aiming himself
toward the outdoor shower.

When he reaches it
with a blind arm
he wrenches the handle
bringing forth a thick stream
of rust-colored water.

The bees halt
confused by this unexpected wall of water
then slowly
start to disperse.

When Helen reaches Joseph
he hands her the child
and then
almost gracefully
he crumples to the ground.

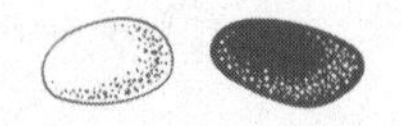

Everyone who saw it
recounts, in a hushed, awed whisper,
how Joseph ran straight for the child,
never hesitating,
how the child was left without
a single sting on its tiny body,
how mere hours later
the many stings spread across Joseph's body
had already begun to vanish.

Helen stares at Joseph
like he is an angel
sent to Earth for the sole purpose
of protecting her child.

And in our cabin
Fern and Poppy
tell it again and again.
The only one of us who
stays quiet is Daisy
who looks not awed
but instead deeply sad.

Willow

WILLOW IS IN THE LIBRARY
tidying the shelves.
She has a system
yet others do not always
abide by it
sticking books wantonly
in places where they have no business.

Daisy had replaced the book
on natural medicines
correctly
but pushed it back too far on the shelf
leaving a dent in the otherwise
smooth line of spines.
Willow shifts it forward
and then, curious,
she removes it from the shelf.

She looks up sage
and then apitherapy.

Learns that sage is used for
nutrients, oral health,
blood sugar, and memory
while bee venom
is used for inflammation, allergies,
and less commonly
for pain, Lyme disease, and dementia.
She flips between the two entries,
trying to understand what ailment connects them.
Then she sees it:
memory, dementia.

She finds herself remembering
first Daisy's strange expression
as everyone spoke about the miracle
of Joseph's immunity to the bees
and then an exasperated Poppy recounting
how Helen claimed Joseph didn't remember her
despite multiple introductions.

Unsettled, Willow picks out another book
hoping to find something to disprove
the thought developing in her head.
Instead, her eyes catch on a term
new to her: sundowning—
an intensification of dementia

in the early evening,
around the setting of the sun.

Her traitorous mind
starts to compile more disloyal thoughts—
of how Joseph didn't join them at the last bonfire
of how curfews have become more frequent
of how Sarah now leads the evening prayer.

She tries to summon her last memory
of Joseph fully present in the evening
and finds a day in the late spring,
mere hours before she'd first reached out
and touched Violet's cheek.

And suddenly, it feels horribly possible
that for all the months of her and Violet being together
this was the consequence,
the insidious toll—
Joseph's very mind the price paid
for her every moment
of illicit joy.

THE GIRL STANDS IN THE RIVER
barefoot
the water rushing frigid
around her ankles
staring at the riverbank
and the mosaic created there.
Earlier, she'd seen Violet kneeling here
but until now she'd not realized her purpose.
It must have taken a long time
for Violet to find stones of the right colors
to lay them out
to form
the words:
You carry my heart
within your heart.

It gives her no pleasure
what she knows she must do
to save these girls from themselves.
It gives her no pleasure
to take a stick
and scatter the stones,

the erasure of the message
the first step
in putting an end to what
has clearly already gone
way too far.

Violet

Violet assumes she's been summoned
to Sarah's office
to talk about perhaps moving the hives
or at least securing them in some way.

She thinks they must be waiting for Joseph to arrive,
so she smiles awkwardly at Sarah as they wait,
but Sarah does not smile back.
Still, she's not worried
until the door opens
and she sees Willow.

Willow sits down,
her hands clasped lightly in her lap,
her eyes upset, distracted
and Violet wants so very badly to hold
Willow's hand in her own,
to comfort her
but they cannot do that here.

Sarah looks at both of them
with tired, knowing eyes,
as if she's seen this,
done this before many times.

You two have been seen together,
Sarah says. *Romantically.*

Violet flinches but to her surprise
Willow barely reacts at all.
No, Violet says, trying to sound calm.
Someone must have misinterpreted
what they saw.

No, there was no misunderstanding.
This is your first and only warning—
which is more than most get.

Violet looks at Willow again,
Look at me, she wants to whisper.
I belong to you, so look at me.

Who told you? Willow asks,
her voice low and far away
as if from the bottom of a well.

It doesn't matter, Sarah says.
The important thing is you tell me
it's over.

Violet looks at Willow
willing her to look back.

Don't say it, she thinks, don't.
Just give me a minute, I'll think of something,
I'll figure something out.

Yes, Willow says quietly.
It's over. It has to be.
She turns to the wall
and starts to gather up her skirt
revealing the lower edge of the scars
anticipating Sarah will reach for the cane.
No, Sarah says. *Not for this.*
You can leave.
Willow drops her skirt
and makes her way to the door
and slowly shuts it behind her.
You can go too, Sarah tells Violet.
I thought you needed me to say it's over first.
Sarah smiles
the type of sad smile
Violet herself has worn
when listening to a child speak
of an impossible wish.
No. It's over now whether you agree
to it or not.
She knows, in the very depth of herself
that Sarah's assessment is correct

that somehow Willow has accepted
the thing she wants so desperately
to fight.
Violet closes her eyes
keeps her head down.
We weren't hurting anyone, she whispers.
Why couldn't you just leave us alone—
haven't you ever been in love?

Sarah sighs. *Child.*
I've been in love
for almost three decades.
But I accepted the rules when
I came here.
And you have to as well.

There might have been a time
when Violet could respond, react to this idea
of Sarah in love
but now she is numb to anything
other than her own pain.

After a few moments
Sarah rises from her chair
and Violet briefly has the strange sensation
of Sarah standing over her,
a hand hovering over her shoulder

then the footsteps continue past her
as Sarah vacates her own office.

Only once Violet is sure
she's alone in the room,
does she begin to cry,
tears streaming down her face
that no one will be brushing away.

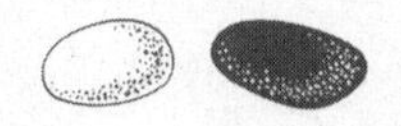

I'M GOING TO SLEEP IN THE BARN TONIGHT,
Violet tells us,
the story all but written out for us between
the puffy skin around her eyes
and the way Willow evades
our questioning glance.

Most of us had long suspected
what the two of them have been doing
and, naturally, we'd disapproved
and yet
this does not feel right,
this severing.

Daisy picks up the cat and gives it to Violet.
Take it to sleep with you, she says.
Violet nods, cradling the cat in her arms.
In this moment
we would all give her a million cats if we could
to knead their heads against her body,
letting their fur absorb her tears.

When she goes,
Laurel asks Willow what prompted this.
Someone told on us, Willow says.
We got caught up in it
forgot there could be consequences
that it was about more than us.

Our sympathies waver
because Violet looked heartbroken, betrayed,
yet still herself
but Willow looks . . . lost
like some essential part of her
has been carved out.
And for the first time
we see the resemblance to Willow's father
the same untethered, haunted look
a cautionary tale
to all who place their fragile
hearts and bodies
in the hands of a single person.

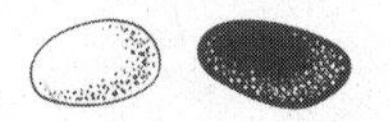

More and more

Rose has started to slip shape in our minds
all the good things coming back:
How kind she could be sometimes
how protective
using her harsh words against others
outside the group
on our behalf.
How she'd tell us stories
whenever we asked her to
even if she was exhausted
ready to be done with the day.

How had we forgotten these things?
How could we have ever thought
she might have intended to leave
this beautiful place?
How could we have ever thought
she didn't understand
how much she stood to lose?

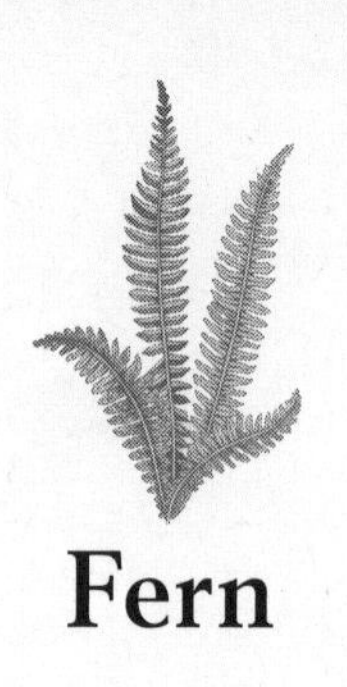

Fern

Fern is up early
alone in the kitchen
assembling small meat pies
firmly crimping the edges of the dough
so that the juices from the meat
do not spill out
and blacken
the sheet as they bake.

If asked
she would not admit
that she'd brushed her hair
much longer than usual
that she is taking care to have a smile
on her face
rather than the frown
she has been told her lips default to.

When she hears footsteps
she makes herself turn around slowly

not wanting to seem overly eager
like Oleanna
desperate for approval
needy.
Joseph smiles at her, eyebrows raised.

I thought I might be the first one here,
he says.

She smiles back.
It's the best time of day to work here.
She takes a deep breath.
It was incredible. What you did for the baby.
There is a flicker in his brow
a small contortion
and a pause before he speaks.

Many things are incredible,
he replies.
If you look at them in the right light.

She nods, and begins to wipe off
her hands.
Coffee, I assume? she says brightly,
wanting to get back onto firm ground.

Yes, thank you.

He wanders over to the counter
staring out the window
deep in thoughts
to which she is not privy.
She takes great care with his coffee

steaming the milk
adding precisely one teaspoon
of sugar and a sprinkling of cinnamon.
She takes it to him
and he blinks, emerging
and after he takes a sip,
he smiles.

I like that taste, he says.
That spice you added.

The cinnamon, she says.

Yes. I've never had it
that way before.
But I always say,
I'll try anything once.

She waits for the beat of a
raised eyebrow
a tweak of the lip
to punctuate the joke.
It does not come.

And she realizes
he truly believes
that this is the first time
he's had cinnamon in his coffee
that this is the first time
the two of them
have ever done this.

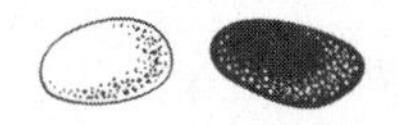

It's a strange thing
how the days can be getting shorter
and yet sometimes feel so very long
like time itself has been forced to drag
a heavy weight.

When we are all back together
in our cabin
the sun is long gone from the sky
and some of us are already
looking toward sleep
with an eager eye.

So when Fern clears her throat
we expect nothing
for the day, surely,
is already all played out.
Yet when we move our weary gaze to her
we find that she looks odd, on edge
and pauses too long for comfort
before speaking.
I think something is wrong with Joseph, she says,
I think he's losing his memory.

The words puncture the room
startling us all wide awake
with their implications
with their audacity.
No, Oleanna says. *That's not possible.*
But then Daisy speaks, her voice soft and measured.
I think Fern's right.
I think he and Sarah are trying to treat it
but it's not working.
We wait
for another of us to cast our decision.
It is Willow who speaks next,
Yes. I think so too.

For some of us
this idea is a new wound
the pain of it
breath-halting sharp
a deep slash into our belief
that we had so much time—
decades
before another—Hamish, Zachary—
might have to take Joseph's place.

For others hearing it aloud
is a firm pressure applied to a slow bleed

bringing a gasp of shock
and then a form of relief.

So what does that mean? Violet asks.
What do we do?

There's a long pause, and then Ivy speaks up.
Perhaps it means
we'll have to begin
trusting our own minds, our own senses
more than we trust his.

This feels like heresy
and we all wait for someone to respond
to reprimand her.

And we wait.
And we wait.
And no one says a word.

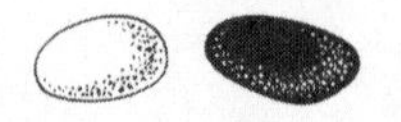

THERE'S A SUSPICION OF AN EARLY FROST
hitting later in the week
so everyone is asked to abandon our regular chores
and go to the orchard to pick apples.
We've taken the rows at the far back,
so we don't have to listen to the others,
some of whom grunt or whistle as they work
in an irritating way.

When a child runs out from the woods
to the base of Poppy's tree,
calling for her to come down,
we roll our eyes,
sure they have some feud
they want her to arbitrate
or some long-winded story to tell.

We continue picking apples,
only dimly aware of Poppy's descent
until she makes a sound
like a muffled groan,
like all the air in her body
was kicked out of her lungs.

Yet it is the look on her face
that makes us all drop the apples in our hands
and scramble down toward her.

The child looks scared and confused,
and Laurel pulls it away from Poppy
allowing the rest of us to swarm around her.
She stares down at an object
cradled in her outstretched palm.
It's small and shiny
partially covered in mud,
on a chain
that hangs forlorn
down the length of Poppy's wrist.
We instinctively feel our necks
finding there a copy of what Poppy holds—
a key to our cabin.
Rose's key in Poppy's hand
found loose on the ground
shatters our brittle hope
that she might be safe
gone of her own accord.
Her key—our key—
on the ground
instead of safely around her neck
means something went
horribly, terribly wrong.

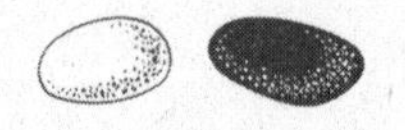

WHEN NIGHT COMES,
we lie down but cannot sleep
a scent peeling off our skin in thick waves
the deep musk of fear.

Do we think it was Hamish? Poppy asks. *That he...*
No, Willow says quietly. *I don't think he could have.*
He said something about having to stay in the infirmary.
Yes, Daisy affirms a moment later.
I saw him there—all curled up.
Clara said he'd been there for two nights.
There is a temporary feeling of relief,
chased by the realization
that this means more uncertainty, not less.

What about Peter? Fern asks.
Could he have hurt her for the money?
Taken it by force?

It's possible, Laurel says,
but I believed him when he said
the money wasn't his.

We fall silent, terrified.
We've been afraid before
but not like this,
we are being besieged
and we don't even know which direction
the attack might come from.
We clutch our keys so tight in our fists
their imprint will be molded
into our palms long after we finally let go,
which may be never,
we may go to our graves still holding them.

A question pierces the black of the room,
slicing it open.
Do we want a gun?
We don't like guns
yet guns have a terrible power,
and after finding Rose's key,
a terrible power of our own appeals.

So, two of us respond to Poppy's question
at the same time:
No, Violet says.
Maybe, Willow says,
like she is trying out that word for the first time,
like her world of certainties has been torn asunder.

We feel it even in the dark,
how both Violet and Willow are shocked
at what the other has said
surprised to find themselves so far apart.
There is a pool of silence,
that grows deeper and spreads,
like oil flowing out across the floor,
rising up to lick the foot of the bed.
We start at the sound of the strike of a match,
imagining the room set ablaze
before a lit candle
illuminates Laurel's face.
We'll have to vote, she says.
And so we do.

Laurel

The sound of Laurel's feet
against the rungs of the ladder down to the shelter
seems painfully loud
despite the soft soles
of her moccasins.

She is not forbidden
exactly
from going down to the shelter
she could claim to be getting a jar of preserves
and as long as she is without a gun in her hand
there would be no reason not to believe her.
Still, it's a relief when she reaches the lowest rung
and can step off onto the dirt floor
where her footsteps are muffled.

Laurel had told the others
she didn't mind going down
into the shelter alone.
It seemed more tactful than the truth:

that she didn't trust any of them
to do it as well as she could.

It smells damp down here
a damp strongly implying the possibility of mold,
of spores settling into one's lungs.
She finds herself trying to take
only shallow breaths.

There are no guns out on display—
but she knows the cupboards to be full of them
and she knows the code to the lock
having once overheard it given
to a boy
much younger than herself.

She begins to turn the dial toward the first number
when she thinks she hears a sound.
She stays impossibly still,
and nothing follows.

Two more numbers, and the lock springs open
and reveals guns packed
from floor to ceiling.

In order to keep their theft secret
they'd agreed to take only a single gun

so Laurel selects one with a wooden inlay
heavy enough to feel substantial in her hand
like she could clock someone with it
and they'd crumble like a marionette.
It's easier somehow to think
of using it that way
than to send out a bullet.

Fern

IVY IS NAPPING
even though it is the middle of the day
so Fern tries to be quiet as she enters the cabin,
shutting the door at half speed.
The light had been perfect
and so she's been taking photos all morning
reminding herself of the glory of the river
of the woods
capturing the wonder of it all.
When she places the camera on top of the dresser
there's a flicker of movement on the bed
Ivy rises up
looking at her with sleep-glazed eyes.

What was that? That sound?

I was just putting the camera back.

Ivy frowns. *Do it again.*

Fern does as asked,
picking up the camera and placing it back down.
It makes a soft but perhaps

rather distinctive clink
as it hits the dresser.

That's the sound that woke me up.

I tried to be as quiet as I could, Fern says,
her desire to apologize fighting
with a growing irritation.

No, that's what woke me up
the day Rose went missing.

Oh. Fern pauses.
Maybe she was deciding
whether to take it with her.

Or maybe she did take it. Like
Madison said she planned to.

But then who brought it back here?
We're the only ones with keys.

Yes, Ivy says slowly. *We are.*

Violet

As Violet walks into the woods
she swings the cloth bag,
letting it gently hit against the side of her leg.
She hopes when she emerges
it will be filled
with late-season chanterelles.
She hums to herself,
trying to break up her thoughts
which keep sliding
toward Willow
as if on an angled slope.

Almost an hour passes
with her only trophy a long scratch
from an errant branch.
Then she is rewarded with the sight
of the yellow flesh
and delicate edges of a chanterelle.
She plucks it from the earth
and scans around it for other ones

spying another half-hidden by a fallen leaf.
Her success makes her giddy
pushing her onward,
deeper into the woods than she'd intended—
and she thrills at the sight of another fine cluster
which one by one
she tosses into the cloth bag.

She's drawing the string of the bag shut,
satisfied by her victories
planning to head on back
when she notices some odd objects
a few yards away.
She blinks, refocusing in the ebbing light,
trying to parse their shapes
and starts moving toward them
before she realizes
one has the very distinct shape
of an all-too-human
hand.

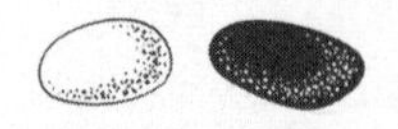

FERN IS THE LAST OF US TO KNOW.
She hears it from Ivy
who hears it from Poppy
who hears it from Oleanna
who hears it from Willow
who hears it from Daisy
who hears it from Laurel.

Laurel is the only one
who hears it directly from Violet herself
who runs out from the woods,
her face gray, her mouth held in a silent scream.
Rose, she whispers into Laurel's neck.
Oh God. I found her. Rose.

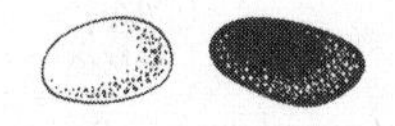

We thought ourselves prepared,
but the scene is so much worse
than what our imaginations pictured.
We find ourselves vomiting on the dark earth
all the food we have ever eaten
leaving our bodies in a sour stream
our stomachs heaving
even after they are completely, utterly empty.
Her body was found by animals
the grave had been shallow
and they had been hungry.

We tie our sweaters around our faces to serve as masks
and work to dig a deeper grave
use downed branches to fill it as best we can
and then cover it with soil and stones.
When we are finished
we look around,
expecting to see animals crouched
behind a thin layer of foliage,
waiting to destroy our work.
We want them to show their faces
so we can charge at them with our sticks,

howling out her name
scream at them
scream at the world

how dare you
how dare you
how dare you.

Laurel

LAUREL WANTS
in a way she hasn't in a long time
for someone to tell her
it's going to be all right
that no harm will be allowed
to come to her.
Wants someone to envelop her in their arms
so she'll feel small and safe,
and sleep as sound
as that cat curled up against Daisy.

She wants
she realizes
to be a child
or rather
to be someone's child.

But the time for that
has long since passed.

She has a new family now
and she is not the only member threatened
so she must be brave
both for them
and herself.

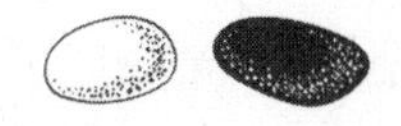

WE ARE ALL IN THE CABIN
when there is a knock on our door.
We look around at one another,
our faces framed in question marks,
for we do not remember
the last time someone came
to our door unbidden.

Laurel is the first to move,
shooting a meaningful glance at Ivy
who leans down, quickly, gracefully,
to retrieve the gun from underneath the bed.

When Laurel pulls the door open,
Helen is beaming at us from the doorway
wearing the dress Poppy made her.
Ivy swings the gun behind her back,
concealing it from Helen's view.
Helen's eyes find Poppy,
and she takes a step forward.

Thank you. It's beautiful.

She laughs—and spins around
the edges of the fabric flying out

brushing against the doorway.
You're welcome, Poppy manages
and Helen seems too preoccupied
with her own pleasure
to notice the woodenness
of Poppy's response.

I know I'll be seeing you at the
ceremony later today, Helen says.
But it's so beautiful that I couldn't
wait to thank you.

None of us respond
all of us hoping someone else
will handle the weight of her joy.

Helen falters.
Sorry. Perhaps this is a bad time?

We attempt to rally.
Oh, we're simply jealous—
Daisy says with a smile.
I know I want one just like it.

Too bad, it's my turn,
Ivy rejoins with a wide smile.
I'm the only one who didn't get a new
one in the spring.
We all look at Poppy,
waiting for her to confirm this
and take her turn at lifting the mood.

Instead she nods—slowly,
like she's almost reluctant to do so.
That's right, she says. *I ran out of cloth.*
But everyone else got a new dress.
And then as Helen leaves
Poppy holds the door open for her
and then
in a strangely bright tone
asks Laurel if she'd care to join her
on a walk.

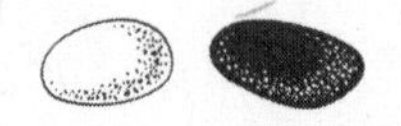

A FEW HOURS LATER

Helen stands in front of all of Havenwood:
radiant, shining.
There's a basket at her feet
and she's wearing the dress,
which fits her perfectly.
She holds her child
yes
but in one arm
its weight against her hip
with a looseness that indicates
she knows they are both safe here
safe enough
to let the child become part of Havenwood
instead of part of her.

She recites the promises
to this place that all those of age
must make aloud
and we can tell how deeply
she believes every word.
That there is no better place
in this world than here.

That nothing it asks of her
could ever be too much.

When she finishes
she goes up to each of us
and offers from the basket
a stalk of wheat
we each smile and take the offered stalk—
accepting her gift
accepting her.
We are all so happy for her
so fully absorbed in the moment
and none of us, none at all
are distracted
by thoughts that burrow and burn
through our minds
branding a path
we will be forced to follow.

Daisy

Daisy is in the orchard,
walking to the infirmary.
Her gaze keeps flickering
toward the woods
she knows she will not be able to see it
in the same innocent light for a long while
that every rustling sound will conjure
not a gentle breeze, or small bird,
but a shadowed stalking figure.
Even in the tidy rows of apple trees
she notices the twisted tangle of tree limbs,
the sour scent of rotting fruit
more than the bright sky.

When she hears her name,
she thinks it a product
of her heightened senses
until it comes again.

Daisy?

She turns to see Poppy and Laurel
standing a few yards behind her.

You've been doing the laundry,
Laurel says.

It's not a question, but still Daisy nods.
Laurel looks at Poppy, who reaches
into the pocket of her overalls
pulls out the photo of them all
in the meadow.
She taps on one of the dresses.

Have you seen this dress recently?
Washed it since Rose went missing?

Daisy is unsure of what is happening here
but she looks at the photo,
searches her memories,
and does not find this dress among them.
No, she says. *But perhaps it is in the closet,*
or one of the drawers.

No, Laurel says. *We've already*
checked everywhere in the cabin.

It could have gotten ripped?
Needed repairs?

Poppy shakes her head. *No one has*
given it to me for that.

Daisy is at a loss.

I don't understand. It can't have just gone missing.

We don't think it did go missing, Laurel says. *We think it was hidden.*

Violet

WHEN THE THREE GIRLS—
Poppy, Laurel, Daisy—
come to Violet
she hesitates at their request
worried about the precedent
of becoming the girl
who shares secrets not meant for others.
I would never have looked in Rose's hiding spot
if she hadn't gone missing, she explains,
if I weren't worried about her.
We know that, Laurel says.
No one will judge you for this.

This hiding place, this secret spot,
isn't in the woods.
It's in the attic of the barn,
where Violet slept that night
sobbing, brokenhearted
the cat kneading itself against her body.

Violet moves lightly on the creaking wood floorboards
stepping over ones that appear uneven
letting her eyes roam
until they catch on a floorboard
that looks wrong to her.
Rest of lines will move up
When she tugs, it comes up easily,
but at first she sees nothing underneath.
She lowers herself to the ground
resting her head on the floorboards
so she can reach in with her whole arm
until she
feels the touch of paper
against her fingertips.
Then she clasps the items
and starts to pull.

What emerges first,
letters in envelopes with smudged ink
addressed to a name
discarded years before
and with them
a snapped lilac rubber band—
a perfect match for the one on the money
that Peter allegedly stole.

She reaches in again,
farther, deeper
and brings back two more items:
a sharp kitchen knife
a dress balled up and heavily wrinkled
    with broad blue-and-white stripes
    and across the bodice and the skirt
        a heavy splatter of dark red brown.

My Dear One,

I broke down and tried to visit you, but I was turned away.

The man, my dealer, who brought you to Havenwood said it was a good place, and in my fog I believed him. Now I am less certain—I don't know if you know that I tried to see you, if you have even received these letters.

In case these letters are making their way to you, and you have the freedom to make your own choices, I've enclosed my address. Please come find me, give me the chance to see your face. If I don't see you, hear from you, I will attempt to visit you once more.

I want—I need—to know that you, my beloved daughter, are safe.

Laurel

LAUREL TELLS FERN
the two of them alone
far away from the cabin
so Fern can react however she needs to
without being overheard.
As Rose's best friend
Fern deserves this courtesy.

It is one of the worst things she has had to do
to sit with Fern
to hear the sounds that break from her body.

Yet afterward
Laurel feels strangely calm.
There is now an answer to the big question.
The infection has been named
and can now be rooted out,
brought into the light.
The rest will simply play out
however it may.

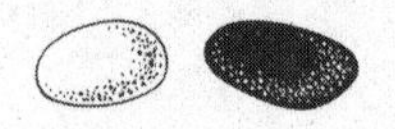

At breakfast
Laurel announces we should go on a picnic later
make sandwiches and take them to the river.
Her voice has a tone of forced gaiety
and it is too cold for a picnic
and yet Poppy seconds this idea
as if it were a beautiful summer's day.

For once, Fern appears utterly uninterested
in arranging the food
so instead Willow packs sandwiches
with tuna salad on whole wheat bread
and slices of apples.
Ivy packs a thick blanket for us
to lay on the bank of the river
and Daisy slings a bag across her shoulders.
Poppy pulls up the mattress and takes out the gun.
In case of wolves, she says.
She is joking, we think,
so we laugh, awkwardly.
She smiles at us,
yet she does not put it back.

The sky is gray and yellow,
the color of storms,
of an unsettled shifting between light and dark.
Much has not been decided.

Poppy carries the gun loosely
almost like how she might carry
a small bouquet of flowers.

When we get to the bank of the river,
Willow puts down the basket full of sandwiches
and Ivy starts to unpack them
but Laurel puts out a hand
and shakes her head
with a finality and resolve
that makes us all become very quiet.
We are not here for a picnic, Laurel says.
We are here because while we still don't know
why Rose was killed,
we do know who did it.
With that, Daisy takes the bag from her shoulder,
takes out a bundle of cloth
and lays it out on the bank of the river.
It is a dress.
A dress we know.
A dress only one of us ever wore.

It takes us different amounts of time to look up
from the dress
to Oleanna.

I didn't see you until breakfast that day,
Willow says slowly. *I remember that.*
I remember waking and not seeing you there.

But that's because she was at
the prayer circle, Ivy says.
That lasts all night.

There was no prayer circle, Willow says.
Hamish seemed confused when I mentioned it,
later said he hadn't missed anything when he was sick.

But the flowers on her hands . . .
Ivy says.

She must have painted those herself, Laurel says.

We picture it
the way it had been almost ostentatious
how she'd combed her hands
through her hair,
the way later in the meal,
she'd modestly dabbed away the paint
with a damp napkin

as if to spare our feelings
but that really only drew more attention.

Why? Fern asks Oleanna,
her voice fierce, her eyes searching.

Oleanna does not meet Fern's gaze
but instead continues to stare down at the dress.
She appears to be considering her response carefully
aware that when she speaks
she will be stepping out along
a tightrope
raised so very high.

It was an accident, she finally says.
I thought she was leaving.
I was just trying to get her to stop.

You used a knife,
Daisy says,
sounding so much less young
than we've ever heard her before.
Oleanna pauses,
her eyes flickering over our faces.
The knife changes things.
She knows that.
We all do.

Oleanna

TWENTY-TWO DAYS EARLIER

MY SLEEP SHORTENED BY INSOMNIA
I'm in the kitchen
cutting a loaf of bread for toast.
Then, through the window,
I see Rose, bag in hand
walking toward the orchard.

I've wondered if it might come to this
ever since I'd accidentally left that floorboard to the side
failing to properly secure my things
and then on my way back to it
seen her coming out of the barn disheveled,
her dark hair
a nest fit for birds.
I'd hoped I was wrong,
but then a few days later I'd followed her,
saw her talk to that girl,
and I knew what had happened:

She'd found the letters from her mother
and she'd been too weak
to resist the entreaties inside.

There is no time to waste
and I leave without so much
as putting down the knife.

Rose is taller, faster than I am
and when I finally reach her, I'm short of breath
and much farther into the woods
than I'd prefer
but I know Joseph needs me to do this
that Rose needs me to do this.

Stop, I call out.
She swings round
startled
until she sees that it's me.

Oleanna, go back, she says.
This doesn't concern you.

No. You can't leave.
You know that.

You don't understand.
This is different.

No, you can't let her lure you away, I say.
She's an addict, and she's manipulating you.

She frowns, utterly without guile.

What are you talking about?

I had been so certain
about her finding the letters
about her plans
yet suddenly I worry
I've made a critical mistake.
So I pivot, play it sideways.
You're off to look for your mom, aren't you?
We've all worried you might someday.

Her face softens. *That's not why—*
Then she stiffens. *Wait. You called*
her an addict. How could you . . . ?

She pauses, running my words
back in her head
wondering how I could know this.

Did she write to me?

I am not used to lying
not in response to a direct question
and I hesitate too long.

She wrote me a letter, and you
didn't tell me?

Look, I say, scrambling to recover,
it's a rule.
We can't pick and choose which we follow.

I expect her to yell at me
to scream
but then
she does something much worse—
she laughs:
a hard, bitter, exhausted laugh.

You're such a pathetic drone that
you probably actually believe that.
But the truth is, people here break
the rules all the time.
As long as it's the right person,
as long as it can be covered up,
it doesn't even matter.

I raise up my hand, angry
wanting her to stop saying such
untrue things.
I've forgotten about the knife.

Her eyes catch on the blade, but
she just shakes her head.
Stop embarrassing yourself,
Oleanna.
I don't have time for this right now.
We can talk when I get back.

There's a crackling inside me
lit by her arrogance in thinking
the rules don't apply to her,

that her future, her soul
isn't at stake.

Rose starts to walk away.
Stop, I say again. *You have to stop.*
If you leave, you can't come back.
Yes, I can. I can and I will.
She says it without even turning around
like I don't even warrant the courtesy
of her saying it to my face.
Like everything
this place is built upon
doesn't even matter.

And so I go, arm raised,
to stop her.
To make her understand
that Havenwood is not a joke
that *I* am not a joke.

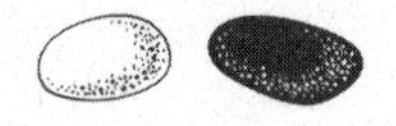

Oleanna's mouth is moving
her protests mere empty noise
as Fern stoops down
and picks up a palm-size rock
her fingers wrapping it so tight
the skin of her knuckles
turns brilliant white.

You killed Rose, Fern says slowly.
Killed her like an animal.

You took the money Sarah gave her
and planted it on Peter
as punishment for his drinking.

You appointed yourself the enforcer,
to keep us all in line
but we never asked for that.

A small sound escapes from Willow
and we shift our gaze to her
wondering if quiet, bookish Willow's intent

is to de-escalate.
But then she speaks, and her words
come out hard.
Was it you? she asks.
Were you the one who told Sarah
about me and Violet?

And we all witness
a flash in Oleanna's eyes
of defiance, self-righteousness
and we know that, yes,
she did that as well
and no,
she is not sorry.

Our pulses race
confronted with the full extent
of the damage she's done:
one dead, one banished
two hearts, broken.
And we remember how—like simple fools,
we had comforted her
after her nightmare—
so sure it was about something
terrible done to her
never thinking it might instead be about
something terrible she herself had done.

Fern picks up a second rock,
extends it out to Ivy.
Ivy looks at the rock, and then at Oleanna.
Perhaps she thinks of the times
Oleanna has braided her hair,
massaged her feet.
But then she takes the rock
and Oleanna flinches,
eyes wide.

Laurel picks up two rocks,
and passes one to Daisy,
who takes it without hesitation.
And with that our decision is made,
and we all pick up rocks.

Oleanna shakes her head,
says we don't understand,
but we understand perfectly:
She is no longer one of us.
Perhaps she never truly was.

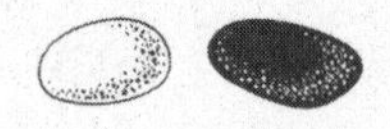

IT DOES NOT TAKE LONG,
it only takes forever.
We throw ten rocks each,
we throw fifty.
The details are not important.

What we know to be true:
that Oleanna is upright,
then bent over,
then down on the ground,
and then
finally, finally
she is still.

What we do not know:
when she stops screaming,
when it is only our own screams
that we hear
coming from a dark red place
deep inside.

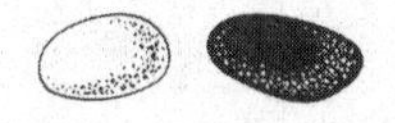

IN A PERFECT WORLD,
we would leave Oleanna's body in the river,
leave it for the animals
and be done.
This would feel like justice.
For us. For Rose.

Instead Daisy and Fern
walk back for shovels.
If we weren't so tired,
we'd be proud of them for this
for having energy still to stand,
to walk back through the woods.

As we wait for them to return,
we lie down on the ground
stare up at the sky.
There are stars up there,
waiting—hidden by the light.

The air is cold
but our skin is warm
together we form a block of heat.

Laurel

Laurel's arms had been sore
her clothes filthy
when she'd returned from the woods
and found a slip of paper
with her name written in pencil.
It had felt like a sign
a benediction.

Now, three days later
Laurel sits quiet and still in the prayer circle,
breathing in and out.
The air smells like smoke and flowers,
and she can taste a hint of lavender in it
and outside daylight is starting to break
bringing the circle to a close.

Oleanna's face
the deep, deep grave
feel like images from a fever dream,

and the fever has since broken
leaving her calm and resolute.

No one has remarked on Oleanna's absence,
but earlier she caught Sarah searching for her,
a small furrow forming in her brow.
Joseph's gaze, however, did not slow
as he looked around the circle.
Perhaps for him
Oleanna has already
disappeared entirely.

When Joseph exits the room,
she finds Sarah watching her
and together they linger
waiting until all others have left.

Oleanna has never missed the circle
before, Sarah says. *Is she unwell?*

Laurel brings a look of regret
to her face, and shakes her head.
Sadly, Oleanna has chosen another path.
She spoke with Joseph about this
at great length.

He did not tell me this.

Perhaps it slipped his memory.
Some things seem to do that now.

Sarah looks at Laurel
her face caught between
a warning and a request.
Then, reluctantly,
she nods.

Yes, perhaps on occasion.
It's possible it could improve though,
she says, her voice suddenly soft.
Possible that it could be a long time
before anything has to change.

Laurel nods in response,
it would be rude to do otherwise.
Still, she wonders
how much time they really have left
before it becomes clear to all
that Joseph will never again be
what he once was
before they will have to work together to ensure
it is Hamish, not Zachary
who inherits Joseph's throne.

Fern

FERN HAS LONG KNOWN
you can fit memories into a little box
inside yourself
even if you have to break them
break yourself
in order to shut the lid tight.
Known you can put that box
on a high shelf in a small room
inside your mind
and turn off the light.
That this is the way
to prevent unexpected shards
digging into the softest,
gentlest parts of yourself.

She explains this to Violet
when Violet tries to talk to her
about what they did.
Explains that what happened at the river
is something she has already put away.

I don't think I can do that,
Violet says.
I'm not sure if I want to.
I think I have to remember.

Violet delivers this with an apologetic look,
as if worried Fern will
take this as a critique.
Fern doesn't though,
it is not a skill she wished for,
simply one she was forced to develop long ago.
She came to Havenwood
with a tall stack of boxes inside her
and this is just one more.

Violet

IT IS NOT NIGHT, NOT YET MORNING
as Violet walks across the fields
the sky kitten gray,
with no moon in sight.

She carries a small canvas bag
over her shoulder
and with each and every step
she questions what she is doing.
Part of her wants nothing more
than to turn back around,
to rip up the note she left
to go tend to her beloved bees.
It scares her to know
how easily she could do that
to decide she truly will pay any price
in order to stay.

To make herself remain on course,
she plays a loop in her head,

of Oleanna's face
as they picked up the rocks,
of Rose's lifeless hand
in the woods
of Willow's expression
as she gave Violet up.

The farmhouse is visible in the distance,
its windows dark.
She has no illusions
that she is heading toward something easy
and if she lets herself
she will be overwhelmed
by how much she does not know,
by how little she has.

She closes her eyes and pauses,
breathing in and out,
in and out,
and when she opens her eyes again,
one of the farmhouse windows is lit.

In that window
she begins to see a new life
start to unfold for herself
and Havenwood begins
to turn into a story,

of a dark, magical place
she had to leave in order to become
simply a girl,
simply a person,
again.

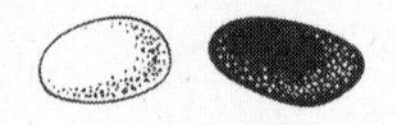

NOT MANY ASK,
but for those who do,
this is what we say about the missing girls:
that they wanted to explore the outside world
despite how, even as they packed,
we warned them
that nowhere else was safe
that nowhere else would they be saved.

We say they all left together
walking toward the road,
hand in hand
and if anyone notices
that our timeline is off,
that all three girls did not leave
at the same time,
they do not say so.

Instead, some sigh and whisper
a useless prayer for these girls' souls,
while others look at us
with a glint in their eyes,
calculating we've turned brittle

a fragile cluster of girls
they can break off one by one.

We look back, our gaze steady
confident we're stronger than ever before.
We know now we can love Havenwood, love Joseph
but also keep our own counsel,
and not hesitate to do what is needed
to protect ourselves, our sanctuary.

For we've learned something about ourselves,
something we should have realized long ago:
that while we are girls,
we are also wolves.

Acknowledgments

Thank you to my agent, Jim McCarthy: You were one of my favorite agents even before you became my agent, and I'm so delighted that I got to work with you on this book—it was a true pleasure.

Thank you to my editor, Margaret Raymo: It has been such a wonderful experience working with you, and you've made this book better and better at every juncture.

Thank you to my lovely beta readers, Ann Foster, Julie Kelleher, Kate Marshall, and Maxine Kaplan: I was nervous that you were all going to hate it, and I'm so glad that you didn't. If I failed to take any of your brilliant suggestions, I'm very sorry, that was obviously a terrible oversight on my part.

Thank you to everyone in my Monday Night Write group: Thank you so much for being such a great group and for managing not to look too horrified when I told you that I was going to take my seventy-thousand-word prose work in progress and try transforming it into a novel in verse. It meant a lot.

Thank you to Ragdale: I received the offer for this book during my residency, and I can't help but feel that Ragdale's magic played a significant role there. Also, I really, really enjoyed the food—Chef Linda, you are a true gift and probably the reason why I didn't get scurvy over the winter.

Thank you to my parents: You are both such lovely people, and I'm so lucky to have you as my parents.

Thank you to my sister, Emma: Thank you so much for reading another of my weird little books. I think you are a really cool and kind person, and I'm so very glad that we're sisters.

Thank you to my husband, Kevin: You continue to be my favorite person in the world, and I love you so much.

• • •